Soul Bound to Scotland

R.L. Dubbert

To Maddie

I hope you enjoy this book.

Cover designed by R.L. Dubbert
Stock media provided by lotus_studio/Ponds5

R.L. Dubbert
Visit my website at www.rldubbertauthor.com

Printed in the United States of America

First Printing: October 2018
R.L. Dubbert, Independent Published

ISBN: 9781717946393

This book is dedicated to my husband and children:
Without you my life would be without color.

Other Works by R.L. Dubbert

All I Will Ever Need, Book 1 of the Datzen Series

Escape from Covenant Cove, A Novelette

Available at Amazon.com in eBook and paperback

Soul Bound to Scotland

.

Part One

Chapter One

Gabriella

I make my way out the front door as I hear Jacob yelling, "MOM! MOM! Dad says we will be there in three hours! First thing I want to see is the giraffes! On YouTube, they show people feeding them and their tongues are so long and black!" He is talking loudly and a mile a minute. Daniel and I had not taken a trip since the birth of our children. This would be our first real vacation. We decided to wait until they were both old enough to enjoy it and remember these moments that will last them a lifetime. Matthew will be seven in September and Jacob will be five next week, a good age to start making memories of our time together as a family.

My husband shuts the hatch on our suburban and yells, "Load up!" The boys dart across the lawn and jump into their seats. Daniel double checks their seat belts, while I checked the lock on the front door. Halfway down our walkway, something made me pause a moment and take in the scene of my family. My heart swelled with love seeing their joy, exuberance, their laughter, before continuing down the path to the waiting SUV at the curb. I slide into the passenger seat, Daniel turns to me smiling like a kid at Christmas, "This is going to be a fun trip and the weather couldn't be more perfect."

I smile back and say, "I know, I was worried about the weather, but you are right, it couldn't be more perfect...let's go!" Daniel was right. I looked out my window to a vivid cerulean blue sky with light wisps of clouds in the distance. The temperature was a warm eighty-one degrees after a cool front passed through the night before, lowering the humidity. It was a beautiful day for early June in Missouri. Normally by this time, the weather went from a bone-chilling frigid winter to a hot scorching summer, but today...it just couldn't have been more perfect. As we pull out of the drive I catch sight of the most stunning white dove sitting on the peak of our roof. The vivid crimson tips of its wings, an illusion caused by the sunlight glinting off the neighbors' red car drew my attention. I watch in fascination as it flies across the sky ahead of us.

Ten minutes later the boys are singing along to their favorite YouTube character, 'We're going to the zoo, would you like to come too.'

"The kids are going to enjoy this," I say to my husband and best friend. This man and I met in kindergarten, fell in love in junior high, and have been together ever since. During our third year of high school, we both decided to join the Army for two reasons. One we were passionate about serving our country and two to help with college expenses. We both enlisted during the school term, him as a fiscal management technician and I chose a career in nursing. The summer after our junior year he stayed in Missouri and I flew to South Carolina for basic training. The following year we spent making big plans for our future. Back then our plans were all laid out or, so we thought. We were married the day after graduation in a small, simple Catholic ceremony with our closest friends and family. After my father passed away, we didn't attend church as often as we should, but regardless, my mother made a promise to him, she would see to it my sister and I wed and were blessed in the faith. Thankfully, our town had a small chapel which partnered with the larger cathedral in a bigger city an hour away that allowed us to have a simple ceremony. The priest, who understood our rush, agreed to marry us before we both shipped out. He performed a condensed version of the ceremony while an older woman I did not know sat at the piano playing softly.

The vibrant red cardigan she wore over a pure white sheath dress caused her to stand out to me. For some odd reason, her appearance engrossed me. The songs and beautiful melodies she played were unlike anything I'd ever heard from a single instrument. When she lifted her gaze to meet mine, her eyes were the most brilliant shade of sapphire blue I had ever seen.

Two weeks after we graduated high school we separated once again, he left for South Carolina and I flew to Texas to begin our advanced individual training in our chosen military occupations. The first year of our enlistment proved to be a difficult separation. Thankfully, Daniel eventually moved to Fort Sam in Texas, where my studies were taking place. We had little to no time to see each other as most of my free time I spent with my books. Our second year, given our marital status, we were both sent to Fort McCoy, Wisconsin, where we finished our Army commitment. We agreed to not sign up for another active duty stint but start to settle.

Within a few weeks of leaving military life, we bought a small two-bedroom single story home on the outskirts of our hometown. Daniel took a position with a local CPA and later bought the business when the owner retired. I went to work at a long-term care facility in the next town over as the evening shift charge nurse. The next year, though we planned to wait a while longer, we found out we were expecting. After a long discussion and pouring over our financials, we mutually agreed, I would stay home to raise our new baby boy, Matthew, and Daniel would become our sole provider. Our plan, at the time, when Matthew went to kindergarten I would return to work. However, two years later Jacob arrived and once again our plans changed. Now we were back on track with our original path. Both boys would be in school come August and I would be starting at the County Health Center in September doing well-baby checkups.

As we drove toward our destination our vehicle filled with pure childhood excitement for our first family trip. The boys in the backseat were exuberantly discussing all the things they wanted to see, touch, and feed. Listening in on their conversation with equal excitement as it played out between them I felt so blessed. Daniel reached across the vehicle grabbing my hand lovingly. I turned toward his smiling face as he looked into my eyes and said, "I love you." That was the last thing I remember before everything went black.

Three weeks later

I'm walking along a well-packed gravel road, taking in my surroundings. The area around me appeared dull with a blue haze over it, like right before a summer storm is about to burst loose. I turn in a circle to examine the sky and glance back in the direction I came from. I see Daniel and the boys are standing together off to the side of the road, the sun streaming through the trees so brightly behind them that it almost blinded me to look at them. My eyes started to adjust, and my vision became clearer, I could see they were waving at me, I smile and wave back. I could barely take my eyes off the three of them standing there, but for a second, my sight caught on a rose bush in full bloom with the most brilliant shade of red roses. I wonder where I am going and don't know why I would separate from them, yet I must go. "I love you!" I call out to them and Daniel blows me a kiss, smiles, but says nothing. Tears begin streaming down my cheeks as I turn to walk away from them. Why am I crying? Why am I leaving them? I don't want to leave them, but something is pulling me in the opposite direction, away from the light...away from my family.

One month later

I start to become aware as I awake from a deep sleep and realize I am in complete darkness. My ears pick up a faint, steady beep...beep...beep, as well as a rhythmic gushing of air. Both sounds are progressively getting louder or drawing closer. Or am I moving toward them? I can't open my eyes and my body feels like I am stuck in concrete. I try to take in a breath, but something... is...not right. I try to talk, but I can't. My heart is thumping with the onset of panic starting to build in my chest as the beeping noise becomes louder and picks up in speed. From somewhere in the distance I hear my sister pleading fiercely, "Gabby?! Gabby, can you hear me?" I can hear her, but I can't answer her. "Mom, go get the nurse! Gabby, hold on, mom is going to find someone to help!" She sounds emotional and panicked. What is that beeping noise? I recognize it, but I can't for the life of me figure out where I heard it before. My heart is pounding out of my chest with the growing panic and I feel out of control. I can't draw in air and the need to do so is overwhelming to me. At last, I manage to open my eyes to a blindingly lit room with the walls painted in the palest shade of blue. The first thing I can visualize is my sister, Diana. She is trying to speak soothingly to me, but I hear the panic in her voice.

"Gabby, you have to calm down! It's okay sweetie, everything's going to be all right!" I fight to take in my surroundings and notice an older, white-haired woman in a dull silvery colored blouse standing behind my sister. My eyesight is fading in and out, but my mind registers the vibrant red trim on the woman's top. As I force my eyes to focus on her face, she is staring back at me with the most intense, sapphire blue eyes. She seems familiar to me, although I can't recall who she is or how I know her. A sense of calmness flows through me as she smiles kindly at me. A dark-haired woman dressed in drab green scrubs moves into my vision next to my bedside. The woman in green says something to my sister, but I can't understand what she is saying. A syringe appears in her hands. I watch her put it into a tube next to my head. Within the span of two heartbeats, a drug-induced fog enveloped me. I'm certain I am not asleep, but I feel- as though I'm floating. The nurse and Diana are talking to me, but I can't understand what they are saying. Where in the heck am I? Where is Daniel, my kids?

∞ ∞ ∞

Next day

The next time I open my eyes, a young dark-haired man is sitting next to me. "Gabriella, can you hear me?" I try to talk, but again everything feels wrong, so I nod my head which sends the room spinning like a top. He touches my hand with his icy one, "My name is Doctor Rodriguez. You are in St. Patrick's Medical Center." What!? I am in the hospital. "You are currently intubated. Do you know what that means?" I focus on his kind face and nod my head as questions are erupting in my mind. "We are going to remove the tube." He goes on to explain the process. I am still stuck on being in the hospital. What happened to me? Where is Daniel? Where are my kids? The last thing I remember is...The doctor begins to pull the tube and all thoughts vanished. The sensation of burning and coolness simultaneously are the only thing my mind is registering before a red haze clouds my vision. I take in a deep lung full of air that burns like acid down my throat. The doctor, as well as a nurse I didn't notice before, are both watching me carefully. She keeps glancing at the monitor and I realize it's to make sure I don't go back into distress. My mind is still reeling trying to process anything and everything that is happening around me. My deepest concern though is where my family is. The last thing I remember...we were going to the zoo, Daniel saying I love you, then nothing else. No, we were walking on a strange gravel road, but I was sure I dreamt that.

The doctor asks, "Do you know who you are?"

I barely nod my head and try to answer, but my throat is so raw, words won't come out.

"Do you know what happened?" He continued.

I shake my head no. I want to ask my own questions and I try, but again, not a single sound makes it past my lips.

The doctor and the nurse make eye contact, something unsaid passes between them, whatever it is, it doesn't look pleasant. Doctor Rodriguez looks down at me with sadness, regret, and something else in his eyes. "Mrs. Fairmont has lost so much," he says to his assistant.

I wanted to yell at him, 'What did I lose?' but the pain in my throat held me silent. His shoulders visibly slump, and he squeezes my hand. Quietly and calmly, while looking at the nurse, he fills in the blackness as a heart-wrenching scream tears from the depth of my soul, echoing through the room.

Chapter Two

Gabriella

One year later

Are you sure this is what you want to do Gab?" my sister, Diana, asks me for the millionth time as we put my suitcase in the back of her blue Ford Escape.

I let out a heavy sigh, nodding my head as I answer her. "Yeah, I think this is something I need to do." Over the last couple of months, I sold most of our stuff or donated it to a local church association to help the community. I packed a few precious things away; such as baby books, our wedding album, and a few little keepsakes I thought I might want to see again someday, storing those at my sister's home. In an attempt to escape the emotional pain, I sold our family home as well. The memories that house held broke my heart and I couldn't stay there alone.

I woke up in a hospital bed to find out, not only the love of my life, but our two boys had died in a car accident. For a month I laid unconscious in a coma while the world went on around me. In some ways, I suppose being oblivious through the pain was a good thing. My injuries, particularly my broken leg, arm, and ribs, had nearly healed by the time I awoke. Hell came with the months of physical therapy that followed to rebuild lost muscle mass. The worst part of it all, I lost the opportunity to say goodbye to Daniel, Matthew, and Jacob. They were gone...forever!

I recalled seeing them on a gravel road waving at me. I wondered later if I had died, but came back to life, or if my subconscious gave me one last time to see them, in a dream. It felt so real, that much I remembered. I didn't ask about it and nobody offered much information on how bad a shape I was in when they life flighted me to St. Patrick's. Thinking about my time in the hospital, no one directly told me anything, what I knew came from bits and pieces I picked up from their conversations with one another. If the scarring in my hairline gave any clue, it wasn't good. In fact, the trauma had been bad enough my beautiful, long, chestnut brown, hair had been cut off leaving me with a pixie cut. A very cute cut, and I tried to view it as a new style for my new life, but I didn't want a new style or a new life, I wanted my family back.

Grief overwhelmed me for over two months. I couldn't get out of bed, I didn't want to eat, I wouldn't see anybody, and under no circumstances did I want to talk about any of it. The physical therapist came to my house three times a week for three months to make sure I did my exercises. Looking back, how I managed to recover I will never know because I never did anything she told me to do. As far as I was concerned I was dead, waiting for my body to figure it out. In our last session, before she left, I apologized to her profusely. I made her life hell when all she did was try to help me. She had smiled and told me, "It's all part of the job, don't worry about it."

At the four-month mark, I called the county health clinic to explain my reasoning for not showing up for the position they hired me for. They assured me they understood and hired a temporary staff member to fill the opening after hearing about my accident. I felt grateful for their kindness, as I knew I wasn't going to be able to keep my emotions under control while working with the young children. The clinic manager surprised me with her empathetic words and understanding. She explained to me the temp she hired wanted to stay on full-time. A sense of relief at hearing this news came over me. I genuinely wanted that job, but for now, I couldn't do it, I didn't know if I would ever be able to work with children again. All I really wanted at this moment was to be alone.

The grieving process is an emotionally trying time. One minute I am in a puddle on the floor begging to have my life ended so I could be with my loved ones. The next minute I found myself standing in a graveyard screaming at the man who left me behind, taking my kids with him. All because he wanted to say I love you. The caretaker at the cemetery, a kind older gentleman, a friend of my mother, witnessed my meltdown at the graveside and called her to come to pick me up. The wonderful thing about a small town is almost everybody knows everyone else and is always there to help lift you up. This pleasant man, in his late sixties, sat at the grave site with me and rocked me until my mother arrived. I would say this was the point I hit rock bottom. I didn't think I had been bottling up my emotions, until the incident in the cemetery. I was so angry with Daniel but angrier for being left behind to pick up the shattered pieces of my life and trying to move on...alone!

After about six months, I started donating random items, such as toys and clothing. Since waking up, this was the hardest thing I had done. I would drop various things off, make it two steps back toward my van, before turning back around, bundling it all up, and heading back home. I couldn't handle the reminders around the house anymore, but I didn't want to part with their things either. I slept on the couch because crawling into bed alone was emotionally painful. I didn't dare go near the boys' room at all! Their door remained shut and I didn't know if I would ever be able to open it again. After three failed attempts to take stuff in for donation, I asked my mom and sister to come to take the things I gathered to the church collection box. Most of the boys' clothing I had bought for the coming school year and was brand new. I wanted, no, I needed to know those clothes were going to local kids who were in need. It gave me some peace, but I couldn't do it myself.

Seven months after I left the hospital I began to get comfortable with my life, my new, all alone life. Still not in a good place, not by a long shot, but I was getting there one day at a time. My world lost its color when I reawakened, everything I looked at appeared drab and lifeless. I supposed my depressive mood altered my perception of my surroundings. I felt drab, so my surroundings became as such. I would drag myself off the couch every morning, sometimes eating two meals a day. While I received a few visitors, I found most people stayed away or sat in awkward silence not knowing quite what to say. What could they say? What should they say? I never realized, 'I'm sorry,' only goes so far and you can only stand to hear it so many times before it becomes utterly annoying. I knew they all meant well and worried over me, but their worry and caring were meaningless to me. The nights were the worst as it was too quiet, no one needing another trip to the bathroom or asking for another drink of water. No pillow talks with Daniel, no arms to hold me or soft snores beside me...nothing but silence. I would close my eyes and they would be there, waving at me, fading into the blinding light. I cried myself to sleep every night, praying for it to all end, so I could be with them.

Chapter Three

Gabriella

Eight months, three weeks, and two days after the accident, the life insurance checks came in the mail. Daniel, always the one to be prepared, took out a $750,000 policy when we bought the house to cover expenses should something ever happen to him. Each boy also had a $100,000 accidental death coverage, as well. I remember when we applied for those policies. I told Daniel it felt morbid to take out such things on your own children. He agreed, but explained, should something ever happen to one of them, the money would help cover expenses we would not normally be prepared for.

I sat staring at those checks haphazardly tossed to the coffee table. The longer I looked at them the angrier I got. This grand total of $950,000.00 was anything but grand. Money, of any amount, wouldn't replace what I lost, my family, my reasons for being, my reason for living. These pieces of paper couldn't bring my husband or my boys back to me. Daniel and I paid off our mortgage early, so that wasn't a concern. The auto coverage on the SUV took care of the payoff for it as well as what little we owed on my minivan. For some inexplicable reason, the check for the vehicle didn't bother me like the life insurance checks did. I worked it out in my mind, the suburban was an inanimate object and easily replaced, therefore that money was insignificant. These checks though, they were for lives, my family's lives, whose lives were more significant than anyone could imagine. The emotional pain of even considering taking them to the bank proved more than I could bear. In my mind, cashing them meant they wouldn't come back, the accident really happened and nothing I could do would change it.

It took Diana two weeks to convince me to put the money in the bank. I filled out the deposit slip and placed all three checks in an envelope, sending my sister to take care of the dreaded deed. I couldn't bear the thought of the cashiers look of pity when I handed her the deposit. While Diana took care of my errands, I sat on my couch contemplating what I would do next. With the drapes pulled shut, the room plunged into darkness with a single sliver of sunlight managing to peek its way through a crack between the two panels. I stared at the beam of light as dust motes appeared to sparkle and float in the ray, like little fairies. Lost in the fascinating scene before me, it came to me, I knew what my next step would be and where I wanted to go.

Diana burst into the house after completing the errands I sent her on, pulled open the curtains allowing the sunlight to pour into the room and yelled, "Enough! You must pull yourself together. Daniel would not want you sitting here wasting away. I know you are hurting, I know you want them back and if I could give you them I would."

I cut her off with a whisper, "I'm leaving."

She stopped mid-rant and whirled to face me, "What do you mean?" her face etched in concern.

I knew what she thought I meant from the tone of her voice. "Not like that! I decided to put the house on the market while you were out and am selling the minivan. I am going..." I hesitated for a few minutes because I knew my sister would throw an absolute fit when I told her my plan.

"You are going where?" her tone filled with concern as she sat across from me.

"I am going to Scotland."

Her eyes went as round as saucers. "Scotland! What the heck are you going to do there?"

I roll my eyes at her animated response. "Live...Maybe I will be sucked back in time while spinning at the stone circle, you know, be whisked back in time into the arms of a dreamy highland laird." I try to make a joke in referring to a book she, our mom, and I read over the winter last year.

She gave me her signature half lipped smirk and quipped, "If he has a younger sexy brother, you send him back here to me. Deal?"

I laughed a little, not the laugh of my past, but a laugh all the same. I explained my choice, "Seriously though, I have wanted to go to Scotland ever since I did a research project in high school about the country. From the pictures I saw, it is beautiful, and there is a lot of history there. I can't explain it, but I have this... overpowering feeling like it is where I need to go." I place my balled-up fist over my heart.

She wrinkled her nose, "You can keep all the history."

She always hated the subject in school, while I always found it fascinating. I explained to her a few weeks ago, before the checks arrived, I checked on a vacation to the Highlands of Northern Scotland, out of curiosity. "I think I will go, but I am not scheduling one of those packages. I'm simply going and will figure out the rest when I arrive." I tell her.

She sighed heavily, "Well, I think it might be good, except for the fact you will be going alone unless you're taking Mom?"

"No, I am not taking Mom! I think I need a walkabout."

She looks at me in confusion, "A what-a-what?"

"You know...a trip to find me. For as long as I can remember it was Daniel and me, then us and the kids. I think it's time for me to find...well...me." I attempt to explain what I mean.

She nods in understanding, but says with concern, "You sure you will be alright doing that?"

Resolved in my decision, "Yeah, I think it will be good. I need to get out of here, away from the memories and the daily reminders. I miss them, terribly and no matter what I do, I can't bring them back, they're gone." I finished on a choked whispered.

Diana nodded slowly and moved in to offer me a comforting embrace, "When are you going?"

I considered this a moment, "After the house sells. I may need to stay with you for a bit if you don't mind?" I knew she didn't. Matter a fact, she had been trying to persuade me to move in with her for a few months now, but I thought I needed to be alone...to wallow in my sorrow.

"W-eee-lll," she began to drag out, "I guess if you don't have anywhere else to go, I can take you in. Or you could stay with mom." She said in a playful tone as she bumped my shoulder with hers. I loved my mother with all my heart, but to move back home now...I couldn't do it.

"Maybe I will sleep in the van out on route ten if you don't have room for me," I said in mock seriousness.

Diana wrapped her arm around my back, "Nah big sis, I always have room for you." I couldn't stop the giggle that burst from my chest.

I was going to Scotland. There were no words for me to convey any sense of logic in my decision, except I felt an overwhelming desire to go. Whatever was there...pulling me there...would heal my shattered heart, I just knew it.

∞∞∞∞

Six months later, over a year since the accident, I found myself scared and boarding a plane for Scotland. Except for basic training, my travels never took me so far from home, definitely not alone. Several times I considered turning around and going back, but I pushed those thoughts away. Aside from my mom and sister, I had nothing left in Missouri. My house sold two months after I put it on the market. I set up a power of attorney naming Diana as my legal executor. I made changes to my life insurance policy dividing the payout between my two remaining family members and added both to my bank account. In secret, I also paid part of my sister's tuition for the next year while she finished medical school with the college funds Daniel and I had set up for the boys. Well, not a complete secret, I told my mom what I did. My sister always dreamed of becoming a pediatrician. I wanted her to fulfill her dream without financial stress dragging her down when she completed her schooling. I also met with Daniel and my investment adviser, changing some of the our...my investments and adding more funds to others. Financially, if I led a moderate lifestyle and watched my spending I would be set for life. I wouldn't need to worry about work, I could enjoy, or at least try to find joy in my life without stressing over money. I would just be doing it alone.

One year and a month ago my life took a horrifically altering turn, but now I was determined to keep on living. The gut-wrenching, 'can't go on pain' that gnawed at me at the beginning of this tragedy was not nearly as bad as it had been. I still had days, but not like they had been, of uncontrollable crying or outbursts of anger. Getting out of our house would help, going to Scotland whether for vacation or to stay would be a new pivotal turning point in my life. I would give it my all to move on from the pain and at least try to overshadow the utter destruction of my soul by creating a new life...a different life.

Chapter Four

Gabriella

Once I made it off the plane and to the hotel, I began wondering if I had made the right choice or not. There were people everywhere, they were inconsiderate, in a constant state of rushing, and rude, moving past me as if I didn't exist in their bubble of space. All I believed Scotland to be, all the pictures I saw, depicted brilliant colors of, greens, reds, blues, and yellows and friendly people. Looking around, I found the intensity of the hues in my surroundings muted and held little luster, like the thick layers of clouds overhead were filtering everything out making it all drab. One building in particular, caught my attention, the facade at a glance, appeared to be a medium shade of brown. However, as I drew closer I noticed the red color faded so much over time giving the building the appearance of being brown. I couldn't help but think it was odd, the building itself didn't appear to be more than a few years old.

I raised my eyes to the overcast sky and mused, this must be a sunless season, as nearly no sunlight managed to peek through the thick layer of clouds blanketing the skies. What I saw was not what I had envisioned Scotland to be, at all, which I found a little disappointing. I knew Edinburgh held a lot of history, which was clear in the famed Edinburgh castle and the cobblestone streets. I took in the sights before me as I meandered down the walkways back to my hotel. The castle held the magnificent beauty I expected, and I was glad I had taken the opportunity to take the tour. However, I didn't feel the edge of excitement I thought I would when seeing it all in person. "Because there is no one to share it with," I muttered to myself as I entered the hotel restaurant.

My waitress, a petite kind woman, around my age, with beautiful, soft, blue eyes, at the quaint little eatery, looked like someone I could speak to about my disappointments. She sat my salad down and asked how I was enjoying my stay. I mentioned my dismay with the scenery, leaving the rudeness of the people out of my statement. She explained city life in Edinburgh differed greatly from some of the smaller neighboring towns. If I wanted to experience Scotland's best, she suggested I should take the time to go further out, maybe to Dochas, about an hour away.

With nothing but time, I would explore the bountiful glory of the Scottish countryside. I felt like the city sucked the little life I held out of me. I came here to find myself, not get lost in the throng of all the others in the crowded streets. I used the internet cafe in the hotel's guest computer room to find my destination. I looked up the waitress's suggestion of Dochas, a farming community northwest of Edinburgh about an hour's drive away. It sat close to the ocean and appeared very scenic, judging from the attention-grabbing pictures I viewed. Cobblestone streets, old storefronts that looked well-kept and rolling moss green hillsides with patches of wild heather blooming drew my attention. The town didn't have a hotel, but a medium sized B&B, which I called ahead to see if a room was available. My heart filled with inexplicable joy when I reserved a room for one week.

I remained two whole days in Edinburgh seeing various sights and doing some shopping. On the third day, a dreary misty Thursday, I boarded an early bus for Dochas, Scotland. Dochas, the Gaelic word for hope, the one thing I needed to find. What I found in this quaint town is what I imagined this country to be in my mind. However, the colors were still off from what I expected them to be. I decided it must be the constant state of overcast that dulled my surroundings, giving them a hazy, blue appearance.

The town itself was not small, but it wasn't an overly large city either. Much like Edinburgh, it held a lot of deep-rooted history, judging from the stone structures lining the streets. Even though the ocean front lay several miles away, as soon as I stepped off the bus the salty sea air filled my nostrils with a tingly, drying sensation. I went straight back to the B&B to check in and drop off my things before taking off to explore my new surrounds. Aside from a bus station and the B&B, the town had a hardware store, farm and feed supplier, furniture and appliance shop, and a few clothing stores. They also had three pubs and two churches. The bars didn't actually say they catered to certain age groups and found it surprising the patrons tended to segregate themselves. One for the twenty-one to thirty crowds and one for middle-aged adults. My favorite though, the fifty and over pub. I can't say what appealed to me more about this establishment. The patrons were friendly, and I didn't have a constant stream of too young or too drunk men trying to buy me lunch, dinner or pints of ale.

After a weekend of taking in the local culture, I felt comfortable and at home in Dochas. Whatever in my heart called me to Scotland found peace with my arrival in this town. This is where I needed to be, I knew it with every fiber of my being. I decided to stay an additional week, which Agnes, the retired widow who owned the B&B was more than happy to let me reserve. Monday afternoon, while sitting in Mackenzie's pub at a window seat watching people move along the sidewalks. Today's lunch special, haggis, which I still didn't have the nerve to try. Once again, I talked myself out of ordering it, instead, I opted for toast and a small coffee, sat back to observe and absorb the rich culture I am privileged in visiting.

While watching out the front window, my eyes linger on an older man, maybe in his mid-fifties, as he is walking down the sidewalk. At first, it wasn't him that caught my attention, but the intensely red jacket he wore. In the drabness of our surroundings, his appearance engrossed me as I watched him greet passersby on the street. I couldn't pull my eyes away from him. As he enters the pub I am sitting in, right away I feel inexplicably drawn to him and an overwhelming desire to get to know him comes over me. He stood about five foot six and around a hundred fifty pounds. His hair was silver and wiry, but I could picture it a strawberry blond in his younger years, and two days of scruff covered his weather worn face. As he scans the room I notice his eyes are warm and kind with lots of wrinkles, which gives me the impression he is the type of man who finds joys in the simplest of things. Two of the older male patrons turn and exclaim, "Hamish!" He placed his hat on the rack along with his light jacket and moves toward the well-worn bar, where the men are sitting.

"What's doing out on the Douglas estate?" one of the men at the bar asks as he approaches them.

"Ah, the usual, working cattle and trying to find help to bale the hay before the winter hits," he answers.

Their conversation grabbed my attention. Even though I moved away from the farming life as an adult, I grew up on a small farm, helping my dad with the cows, raking hay, and building the fence. Though it was rude, and I shouldn't, I continued to listen in as Hamish tells his woes of trying to find reliable hired help for the fall season. He goes on to tell them about an old servants' cottage he'd be willing to fix up if the right person came along as part of an incentive. He would even be able to let them stay through the winter if they worked out he would also need someone come spring. They boisterously continued about how hard it was to find good help these days and how young people were more interested in what their phone screens held, than honest work.

After thirty minutes of visiting, the man, Hamish, suddenly got ready to leave, explaining to his friends he only ran into town to get some feed and other supplies. My body took over and I jumped up out of my booth as he neared me, "Mister, ah, Hamish, sir. I couldn't help but overhear, you need a farm hand."

He gave me a good once over and smiles as his friends' chuckle behind him. In a light Scottish brogue, he says, "Well now lass, I don't know if you are aware, but the work I need doing can be a bit...well, dirty, and not to be rude lass, but you don't look like the type to do hard labor."

I look down at myself in casual, well pressed, khaki slacks, white Ked shoes, and a light blue polo shirt. I look back at him amused by his assumption, "I may not look like it at this moment, but I do know how to rake hay and hold tails for cuttin'." I fall back into my Midwestern way of speaking as I make my case for hiring me.

He quirked an eyebrow and smirks. "And tell me, lass, what kind of tractor did ye use?"

I proudly answer with my most favorite from my Dad's farm, "An Oliver 1850, narrow front end, gas, with no cab. Cabs and air conditioning aren't for real farmers." I added my father's two cents on air-conditioned cab tractors and what he told everyone, instead of the fact he couldn't afford a new one.

Hamish looked almost impressed. Continuing to smirk he asks, "How do you hold the tail?"

"Firmly, and straight over the back, otherwise the cutter will be kicked in the face."

I answer with the strictest of confidence. In the back of my mind, I am wondering, what on earth am I doing, I haven't worked on a farm in years. I didn't need a job, however, my Dad always said take care to help those around you if you can and this man needed help.

"How much do ye be requiring for pay?" he inquired, looking me up and down again as if he couldn't believe he was considering offering me the position.

"I overheard you say something about a cottage? I will do the work for free if I can spend the winter there."

He looks at me skeptically, "How long are you planning on staying here? You are an American, on vacation, I assume. Are you waiting on money to be sent to get home?"

I understand his concerns but answer him with honesty, "It's a long story, but I can stay as long as you need me. I don't need to be anywhere, money is not an issue, and you could use the help."

He strokes the silvery stubble on his chin, considering my offer. "I will pay you five pounds an hour and the cottage for the winter. I can't say what kind of shape it's in as last year some backpackers decided to take up residence there without permission. They were there for a few weeks before we were able to remove them from the premises." He looks thoughtful again. "If you are free today, I'll take you to out to see it and the estate."

I beam up at him. I am clueless as to what I've gotten myself into, but for the first time in a long time, I am...excited about doing something! "Absolutely, could you give me a few minutes to put on more...appropriate clothing?"

He agrees, telling me he will meet me at the farm supply store down the street. I rushed back to my room and wasted no time changing my clothes. I didn't want to give him time to change his mind about hiring me. When I arrived at the feed mill I decided to go ahead and buy a light pair of rubber boots, or wellies, as they called them here, and a nice pair of insulated knee-high Muck style boots for the colder days. I also buy two sets of leather gloves, pliers with a pouch, and a chore coat, everything a woman would need to begin work on a ranch.

Hamish beamed at me saying, "You really do know some of what you're doing, eh lass?"

"I know a little, probably about enough to get me in trouble." I chuckle as we started for his truck, "By the way, my name is Gabriella Fairmont, but my friends call me Gabby."

He paused, turned to me, and extended his hand, "It's a pleasure to meet you Gabby. I'm Hamish." I smile and giggle to myself thinking 'Hamish Douglas, doesn't get more Scottish than that.'

On our thirty-minute drive from town to the farm, I tell him my story, from the accident to waking up, clear through my arrival at Edinburgh and why I came to Dochas. He tells me about his wife, Molly and how she runs the kitchen, the gardens, and the house, but she isn't much for the cattle work or hay. I always loved working on the farm with my Dad and even though it had been awhile, I knew it would all come back to me.

We stopped by the servant's cottage first. I don't know what I expected, but this was more than a cottage, it was a house. Upon first sight, it looked very quaint with wild heather in white and lilac growing all around the front porch. The exterior walls appeared to be made from hand-cut limestone. The edges weren't all straight and each individual block held its own unique weathered grey appearance, made darker in color as the slow drizzle shifted into a light rain. The roof, which must have been newly covered, was a bright shade of red tin, which offset the age of a stone chimney protruding from the left-hand side of the gabled roof nearest me. It took me by surprise that the red stood out so vividly when everything else lacked vibrant color.

As I followed Hamish through the front door, surprise filled me as I took in a spacious living room with sparse furnishings but found it cozy all the same. The warm beige color walls trimmed out with a light brown stained wood made me feel like I was home. A quick walk through and I found this to be a single bedroom home, with a full bath connecting the bedroom and kitchen. I was thankful for the large bathroom where a regular capacity washer and dryer were tucked into a corner. I hadn't noticed a coin laundry service in town and these would make washing blankets a lot easier. The best part of the house, the antique claw foot tub, it sold me on staying here. As I tried to pull my eyes away from it I couldn't help but think, 'I will be spending a few hours in there at least once a week.'

Entering the kitchen, I found it large enough to have a small work island with a butcher block top in the center. A table with two chairs sat up against the wall with ample walking area around it. The space felt warm and welcoming with the walls painted the color of freshly churned butter, white with a slight creamy yellow tint to them, enough to give you a warm cheery feeling. Off the kitchen, I found a mudroom. Through the glass of the back door, I could see a covered footpath leading to a small out building a few feet away. Hamish pointed out to the building explaining I could find wood and various tools in it.

Considering the entire home, the living room was by far my favorite area. Its rich tones of beige made the entire home warm and inviting with a cozy feel. In the living room sat circulating wood stove, much like the one in my parents' house. Hamish told me the appliances were old and may be contrary, so if I should have trouble with them to call and let him know. With a look of concern on his face, he informed me the cottage used wood heat only and during the winter months electricity could be sketchy. I assured him not to worry one bit as I grew with wood heat and what went with it, which took away the pinched look of stress off his face.

I stood out front taking in the view of my new home. In a thought to myself, I considered the cottage as perfect for what I needed and felt blessed for this opportunity for a new beginning. Hamish interrupted my thoughts explaining three years ago a contractor installed a new metal roof and insulation, so I be plenty warm and dry through the winter. He told me he would send Molly down to clean it up for me, however, I told him not to bother her with the cleaning, I would be more than happy to do it.

Chapter Five

Gabriella

Hamish gave me the rest of the week and weekend to situate myself in my new home, but Monday morning I would begin a new chapter in my life as a ranch hand. He gave me a tour of the property, the cattle working area, and the fields we would be baling. I fully expected to find Highland cattle on this farm but to my surprise, the Douglas's produced red Angus instead. The hay fields were a lot like the ones back home in Missouri, growing full of the sweet smell of an alfalfa clover mix. Perfect for hay, but dusty and itchy to bale. In my younger years, I helped my dad on our farm, it was nothing for me to rake hay while he followed with the baler. We too produced alfalfa and a vision of the plumes of dust that came with the baler across the field burst into my memory. As I looked around this Scottish estate, it struck me how much this place made me think of my Missouri home. If I didn't know I was indeed in Scotland, I would have thought I was looking out over one of my father's hay fields.

We left the field and cattle behind heading to the large house to meet Hamish's wife, Molly. A beautiful, older woman, maybe in her mid-fifties, with silvery-grey hair and striking blue eyes greeted us as we walked through the back door of the house. Her very pleasant, warm, and welcoming demeanor made her seem bigger than her five-foot plump frame. From the moment we made eye contact she gave me a sense of peace. In her presence, I felt like I had come home. Their huge house could almost be considered a small castle in its own right. The entire structure stood two stories and made from the same cut limestone as the cottage. Rather than a red tin, the roof of this house was dark grey, which appeared nearly black in the dreary overcast sky. An expansive addition on the west side of the original house was not in limestone, but stucco style plaster, the same grayish color, as the actual stone.

Molly explained for well over a hundred years the same family held the estate. Prior to that, the property housed the keep of one of Scotland's most prominent clans. She went on to say a few years ago they added on the west wing and conservatory on the east side of the house. However, she didn't give me any further information or the clan name. I made a mental note to ask later. In the pub the men referenced the Douglas estate, so I assumed they were the Douglas's. This place...this land, like everything else in Scotland, emanated rich history. I couldn't have been more pleased with my decision to come here than I felt in this moment.

Hamish offered me one of the farm trucks to drive and I told him I would return the following afternoon to begin the process of cleaning and moving in. He handed me the truck keys and bid me farewell, with a knowing look on his face. At first, I wondered why he looked at me in such a manner, then realization dawned as I slid into the driver's seat to find...no steering wheel. I giggled to myself as Hamish shook his head walking back to the house. I got out of the truck and went to the other side...the passenger side to me, and got in. It took me the entire thirty-minute drive back into Dochas to get the hang of driving, on the wrong side of the vehicle and the left side of the road! I was ever grateful to be in a rural area, for it was much like learning to drive all over again. It required every bit of my concentration. I thanked the good lord above for the automatic transmission in the truck and not a manual, as that would most assuredly been a disaster. I knew how to drive a stick but shifting with my left hand would have completely baffled my mind.

The next morning at the B&B, I discussed with Agnes my new living arrangements and job. "Ah, lass, Hamish and Molly are good people. You'll do just fine in their care," she thought a moment, "but should ye have any troubles, you can always come back here to ol' Agnes." I thanked her for her kindness and the breakfast before returning to my room to make a list of supplies I may need for my cleaning project.

I hit the store buying every possible supply I could find; bleach, glass cleaner, sponges, rags, a broom, dustpan, and mop were a top priority of items I might need. Once I paid for and loaded my purchases, I headed out to my new home to begin the cleanup process with a growing excitement, an emotion that eluded me for some time. As I took in my new residence upon my return, I noted the place could've been a lot worse than what I found. The trespassing squatter took exceptional care of the place, as I could see no real damage.

I began cleaning in the bathroom, bleaching almost every surface and even gave the walls a good wipe down. While in there, I decided to run the washing machine through an empty cycle with bleach. However, the aged contraption would not turn on. I checked the breaker box and found all appeared to be in order, so I went back and unplugged it. I considered calling Hamish, but the idea of buying a new one, in my mind, would be the best solution. With the decision made, I gave the dryer a good once over and opted to make it a matching set.

Finished with the bathroom, I moved to the bedroom to work my cleaning magic in there. As soon as I took down the dingy beige curtains, I regretted it. They were so dusty and dirty, a cloud formed when I lifted the rod from the holders, leaving me in fits of sneezing and coughing. I took the filthy things straight out the back door and dropped them in a trash can. My mouth fell open in shock to see the material at one time had been white, not beige. Judging from the cloud that puffed out of those curtains when I took them down, they had been hanging a long time; another definite purchase. Looking at the bed, I already knew it would need replacing at my expense. There was no way I would sleep on that piece of questionable furniture. The phrase, 'don't ask, don't tell', from my Army days crossed my mind. I wasn't going to ask about the bed and I wasn't going to tell I had gotten rid of it. I completed the bedroom, again wiping down the walls, cleaning the windows, and then sweeping the floor. In the past I didn't care much for hardwood floors, but after the curtain situation, I gave thanks for the lack of carpeting in the rooms. I didn't consider myself to be obsessive-compulsive about cleanliness, but the thought of all that dust in a carpet made me cringe in disgust.

I continued cleaning well past dark. As I completed my tasks, I decided to replace all the furniture and appliances. Some might think me crazy to make such an expenditure on a place I would more than likely leave in the spring, but I felt like Hamish and Molly were doing me a huge favor. Even if they didn't know it, they were giving me the chance to live again and to move on from my pain. Since Hamish insisted on paying me five pounds an hour, I would use that money to update the place. At the end of the day, satisfied with the cleaning, I headed back to town to the B&B, showered, and with a heavy sigh, fell into bed without a second thought.

Wednesday morning, I hit McCleary's Furniture and Appliance Shoppe Plus more. The ' plus more' being linens, dishes, and other goodies to make a house a home. It reminded me of a JC Penney store without the clothing, shoes, and jewelry. As soon as the salesman approached me I asked if they would be able to deliver to the Douglas farm.

He quirked a quizzical eyebrow at me, "Does Mr. Douglas know you are moving in?"

I laughed, a little taken aback by the comment, but remembered the squatters, "Mr. Douglas hired me personally. I won't be in the main house I will be in the servant's cottage along the drive."

He nodded his head in understanding. "Do I need to bill these items to Mr. Douglas?"

I crinkled up my nose, "Absolutely not...what I purchase today will be for my own comfort." The salesman grinned in approval of my gesture. During my cleaning, I found the dryer, stove, and refrigerator were all gas powered. I picked out a refrigerator which ran off both electricity and propane. The salesman explained this was their most popular model due to the duel power option. The gas acted as a backup in case of long-term power outages, which came in handy in this area, as winter ice storms were quite common. I found it to be ingenious and decided to call my mom and tell her to buy one for her home. It was nothing for her electric to be down for a week or more during an ice storm.

The stove, washer, and dryer were easy to pick out. I didn't need anything too fancy but wanted the extra-large capacity washing machine, so I could wash blankets. Then a thought crossed my mind, more than likely the hot water heater needed to be updated too. Taking a cold shower after an exhausting day working didn't appeal to me in the least. Since the store appeared to be a 'one stop shop' I took the chance and asked the sales clerk if they sold and installed new hot water heaters. He stared at me, puzzled for a moment before he guided me to the back corner of the shop, where hot water cylinders were on display. Chewing on my lower lip. I studied the assorted sizes on display, listed by liters, not gallons.

Picking up on my dilemma the sale clerk asked, "How many people will be in the residence?"

"Oh, it's only me."

He continued, "Typically, in a lot of our residential homes, they have a heating cylinder like this. This particular style isn't hard to install, as long as there is enough space." He looked at me with an unspoken question in his eyes.

As I studied each tank, trying to visualize the tank in my mind. I pointed to one. "I think the current one is about around that size."

He chuckles, "That is a hundred and fifty-liter system, which I believe is close to forty gallons."

I had no idea, it could be twenty gallons for all I knew. "That should be plenty."

He nodded and wrote it down on the list of my items, he carried with him. Next, I requested to view their furniture, explaining my need to purchase several things in that department as well. At this point, he stopped me to ask if this would be cash or credit. I understood his concern and did not blame him in the least. If a foreign woman randomly showed up, buying half my inventory, I would question it too. I told him I would be paying in cash. Those must have been the magic words because in a much friendlier tone he said, "Cash today, delivery tomorrow. We can even haul off the old appliances and furniture for you as well."

"Perfect!" I called out before continuing with my shopping. I picked out a super comfortable queen mattress with a basic frame and a simple night stand with a matching dresser, a down comforter, two fleece blankets, three sets of eight hundred thread count black sheets and four standard pillows. I paused a moment looking at the black bedding in my arms, put them all back, and picked up a blue plaid, sunshine yellow, and a soft pale green with tiny flower print. I needed color, I needed to start moving away from the darkness trying to envelope my spirit. Maybe if I brought more color to my surroundings, it would help.

I shook off my internal thoughts and headed for the furniture section with the salesman in tow. I picked out a plush overstuffed couch in hunter green with a reclining chair at one end and a matching armchair, a couple of end tables, and coffee table. He happily totaled my purchases and guaranteed delivery by nine tomorrow morning. I laughed and told him he could have the rest of the day off. He gave an amused chuckle, saying to me, "In terms of sale it was a good day, but it may all be returned when Mr. Douglas realizes you're an American!" What an odd thing to say, I mused to myself, but shook it off and headed out the door.

I stopped back by Agnes's B&B to collect my things and check out. She wished me well and became the second person to make a strange comment about the Douglas's. "Aye, good luck to ye lass. If Mister Douglas gives ye any trouble ye come straight back here to me. I will find ye a bed, even if I have to give ye me own." She gave me a nice motherly hug. After thanking Agnes, I made a quick stop at the local grocery and picked up a handful of items for nourishment. Before stocking up on groceries, I would wait for the new refrigerator to arrive. Even though the salesman said they would be there in the morning, I learned long ago, never plan on something until it happened. When arriving back at the cottage, I opened all the windows to combat the bleach fumes that overwhelm me as I enter the front door.

Later in the afternoon, the petrol company arrived to fill the tank. Hamish instructed him to fill it up for the new tenant and to charge it to the estate. I politely requested a copy of the receipt. I knew Hamish would say it was part of the deal, but I didn't want to give him any reason to believe he allowed a freeloading American to move in, since the people in town showed shock he would allow me near the place to begin with. The delivery man wanted to pressure check the appliances, but I explained new ones would arrive tomorrow morning. The man expressed his relief, saying he thought his Dad, who previously owned the petrol company, remembered the day old man Mr. McCleary installed them. We shared a brief chuckle over that before he gave my hand a shake, saying he was incredibly surprised Mister Douglas would allow an American to live here. For the fourth time today, I wondered why people were so surprised by Hamish hiring me.

"Well, I guess I made a very good case for him to hire me."

He shook his head, "You must be more vicious than you look."

I just smiled and waved as he pulled out of the drive.

With nothing much to do, I decided to begin moving everything out the front door I could, by myself. It was no surprise that I couldn't move most of the furniture, as everything in the place predated the 1980's and was extremely heavy. By the time I had finished, it felt like I moved items around for hours. The thought of sleeping on the couch or the bed made me itchy all over, so I opted to sleep on a blanket on the floor. "Daniel, can you believe this? Have I lost my mind? I miss you all so much and I hope you are watching over me." I murmured to the ceiling before drifting off to sleep.

The next morning the delivery van arrived right on time. Van might be the wrong word. A semi-truck and trailer pulled up, along with a van with six guys inside. They went to work, moving the appliances and furniture out. They started in the kitchen taking out the old stove and refrigerator. I scurried behind them cleaning with as much thoroughness as I could; wiping walls and quick mopping the floors where the old appliances sat. While I scrubbed, they moved out the washer and dryer and I went in behind them. Another set of guys started moving in the fridge and stove. This is how we worked for over an hour. With all the furniture moved in, appliances in place and the water heater installed, they turned on the propane, checking for leaks and pressure testing. As they turned out of the drive, Hamish and Molly pulled in with looks of shock on their faces as they watched the truck and van make its way down the driveway. I hesitated in inviting them in, not because I didn't want them there, but I knew how they would react when they saw all the changes I made.

Needless to say, they both were shocked and a little disapproving of the purchases, not because I made them, but because I spent my own money on them. I kindly explained it wasn't fair for them to pay for my comforts, and while appliances might not be a comfort, constant repairs on those appliances just seemed to me to be more of a hassle. I told them we could settle it up when they fired me. My jovial demeanor seemed to lighten the mood and we all got a good chuckle out of it. Molly, impressed with my cleaning skills, told Hamish she might steal me away to assist her. Laughing he moved her to the door reminding her they had a reservation in Edinburgh. I looked to my watch thinking it a bit early to be leaving for a dinner date, but Hamish explained shopping was on their agenda as well. Their youngest daughter, Sarah, would be having a baby soon.

Thursday afternoon while admiring my new accommodations, I called my sister for a quick update on my status and to find out how she was doing in school. Afterward, I made a grocery list and headed toward town. When I left the house, I saw several downed trees on the perimeter of the property and decided I would pick up a chainsaw and fuel mix to clean up the yard and in the process, stack up some firewood. Last night, it didn't take me long to figure out, it can be cold in Scotland at night, especially after the sun went down. Fortunately for me, I grew up cutting wood, even after dad passed our neighbors would come help cut winter wood for mom. It wouldn't be long until the weather turns dreary, rainy, and icy all the time, I wanted to be ready.

The guy at the hardware store eyed me funny when I told him what I wanted to buy. When he asked why my husband didn't take care of such things. I explained in limited detail my status as a widow starting over in Scotland and my position on the Douglas farm. Before he could get out the American comment I held my hand up, telling him I was aware of Mr. Douglas's feelings toward Americans, but I assured him the man hired me happily despite my lineage. He smiled at me with a knowing twinkle in his eyes before going over the chainsaw with me. Leaving the hardware store, I headed to the grocer. Confident my new refrigerator wouldn't go out, I made a rather large purchase, stocking up to save on trips back into town. I probably picked up a lot more than I needed, but you can never be too prepared, especially in an unfamiliar climate.

Friday, content with my situation and not having much to do, I headed to the main house in search of Hamish. Finding him in the barn, I explained my reason for showing up early and requested to shadow him as he worked. He agreed. I spent that afternoon and Saturday not only watching how Hamish did things but helping him move cattle to the field close to the working pen. Sunday afternoon we took the time to get our equipment ready to work the livestock. We placed new needles in all the syringe guns, made sure they worked properly, and all the medication hadn't expired. We checked the ear taggers, changed the blades in the cutting knives, and even greased the chute and checked the rope for fraying. When we finished everything was set up and ready to begin working cattle the next day.

Tomorrow morning, we would work the cattle, separate the calves for weaning, and give them shots as well. In the afternoon Hamish would cut the hay and I would follow with the tedder increasing our chance of baling it faster. Tuesday morning, we would work with another batch of livestock and hopefully, we would be ready to begin the process of baling the winter hay after lunch. Hamish explained every detail of our work day to me, but grinned slightly at me when he said, "That be if everything goes to plan. Never know when a tractor may break down or a cow decides she isn't going to cooperate." I smiled knowing full well what he meant. I remember my dad always saying, 'God willing and the crick don't rise.'

Chapter Six

Gabriella

Working the animals the next morning got off to a rough start, as it had been a while since I had done anything with cattle. My only redeeming quality, my medical training. As a nurse, I had given my fair share of shots and the injection guns we used were similar to the ones the military used. The only difference being we used an actual needle rather than pressurized air. We stopped for a filling lunch of fried chicken and roasted potatoes prepared by Molly. Afterward, I could have taken a nap, but it was time to move into the hay field.

Hamish pointed me to the faded blue New Holland tractor I would be driving. Taking in the sun faded paint on the tractor, I thought once again, I came when the weather remained overcast. Evidently the sun did shine here at some point. He directed me to the machine shed where the tedder rake was located so we could hook it up. Thankfully, tractors are universally setup, I wouldn't need to spend time figuring out how to drive on the wrong side of the vehicle, but I did need to reacquaint myself with the various gears and levers. Ten minutes later I followed Hamish on his faded green tractor into a huge hay field, at least a hundred acres lay before us. My eyes took in the sites, even though he showed me the fields prior, seeing it again took my breath away. For as far as I could see the land appeared like a green ocean, with the grasses like wild billowing waves rolling in the soft breeze. The light pungent, earthy smell of the alfalfa flashed me back to another time when I was much younger until Hamish began cutting and the scent became almost overwhelming.

Hamish ran his tractor a few feet down the field before I took off. I adjusted the radio, gave him a few more seconds before engaging my PTO lever to start the tedder whirling. As I drove over the perfectly straight lines Hamish laid out before me, the tedder tossed, fluffed, and laid the grass back down like a blanket over the field behind me in the tell-tale sign of an alfalfa dust cloud. As we moved down the rows I felt fortunate the wind blew toward me, keeping most of the dirt behind me until we turned at the end of the row and made our way back across. By the time we finished, a thin layer of itchy, dirty, alfalfa dust coated every part of me. As soon as I returned home I took a quick shower to rinse the grime from my skin and down the drain, before filling the aged claw foot tub with hot water and bubbles. Tonight, was going to be a long soak kind of night.

By the time Thursday rolled around my muscles ached, exhaustion set in, and a day off sounded divine, but we continued to bale hay. I didn't recall farm work being so tiring. As a kid, everything in life felt a whole lot easier than it did as an adult. I shoved those thoughts away as an image of my boys flashed through my memory. I didn't want to open my Pandora's Box of memories, I needed to focus on helping Hamish get the hay baled before the rain set in.

On Friday we began hauling in the hay. Thank the lord above Hamish did big round bales and not square. I believed I kept myself in pretty good shape, but not good enough to stack bales like I did in my teens. I would have done it, but I don't think my body would have much appreciated the extra work. Given my current knotted muscle aches my body already was not happy with riding the tractor all afternoon.

Hamish drove a tractor with the bale fork on the front while I drove a second with a large wagon. He stacked them on my buggy, then I would haul them to the huge barn and unload them with a skid steer, stacking them inside. Hamish explained, after filling the barn, we would stack them beside the alleyway alongside the building. He would feed the bales exposed to the elements first. By lunch on Saturday we had all the cattle worked and all the hay in.

Overall, I thought everything went rather well. Hamish reaffirmed my thoughts when he clapped his hand on my shoulder in a fatherly gesture, saying he sure was glad to have someone who knew what they were doing. He expressed his surprise that we managed to get it all done in a few days' time, giving me the rest of the day off. Hamish instructed me to come back on Monday at seven to do it all again. I smiled at him as I slid into the truck to head home, however in my mind I groaned with exhaustion at the thought.

I returned to my little cottage thinking of all my accomplishments this week, feeling a sense of pride I hadn't felt in a long time. I pondered on that a moment. In seven days, while I still felt the loss and sadness, the overwhelming feelings of complete despair left the forefront of my thoughts. I knew Scotland would be a place for me to heal my shattered soul. As an adult, religion was not a top priority, I had faith and felt it was enough. Daniel, the kids, and I would attend Easter and Christmas mass, but that was about as religious as we got. However, what beliefs I did have compelled me to believe the guiding hand of a higher power led me to Hamish.

Chapter Seven

Declan

After a month-long business trip to the United States, all I could think about was getting back home. I longed to sit in my study and sip an aged glass of scotch without constant distraction. The drive from Edinburgh Airport took a lifetime to travel. As I turn down the long winding path leading to my fifteen-hundred-acre estate, the tension left my body and a peace came over me which I hadn't felt since I left. I loosen my tie and take in a deep breath. I am not fond of extended business trips to the U.S. and less happy to return in a few weeks to finish up the deal. I could have stayed, but I needed to go home and recoup. I longed for my high back, Italian leather office chair and two fingers of the Johnnie Walker Blue Label 1805 I bought at auction. The company only released two hundred bottles of that special blend and I rarely partook of this bottle, but after this trip I needed a little something extra special to welcome me home.

About halfway up the drive, still lost in thought, I sight the red roof of the little servant's cottage coming in to view. Again, I consider contacting a contractor to come and take it down, but I spent money replacing the roof and insulation about three years ago. The contractor made a mistake when ordering the tin and when I returned home to see the vivid red, it was too late. The cottage needed to go, as it tended to draw uninvited squatters. Last year, while away on business, a pair of female backpackers from the States came upon the place and decided it looked like an inviting place to stay. They tried to make a permanent residence for themselves. It took me a month, a MONTH, to run them off MY property! They began spouting nonsense about land ownership being nine-tenths of the law and a myriad of other garbage about a free Mother Earth and global society. After a call to the Dochas Police Department, finally an arrest came, and the police removed them from my property. About a week later those bothersome women in turn contacted a solicitor to file a wrongful eviction suit. After six months of ridiculous suits, the nightmare ended, and I had no intentions of doing it again. "Blasted American women ruin everything!" I mutter to my steering wheel.

As I approach I notice smoke coming out of the chimney, and an older farm truck, my old truck, backed up at the side of the little house by the woodshed. A boy, about twelve or thirteen stood in the backyard with my gas-powered splitter, splitting wood. "You've got to be freaking kidding me!" Anger grips me as this new squatter scenario plays out in my head as I whip into the drive and jump out of my Rover. The boy turns with a look of mild concern on his face and starts to walk toward me with an ax in his hands.

"Can I help you?" he calls out. For a moment I froze in my angry strides. A petite bonnie lass, in her late twenties, stood questioning me. An American woman, not a boy at all! A second passes as my brain catches up with what I am seeing. The little woman comes to a stop about two yards in front of me with a death grip on the ax in her hands. The vision of my six-foot-two-inch frame and anger etched face placed her on a defensive guard, as well they should.

Oh, I don't think so! I gather my wits. She has the audacity to stand on my property, in a threatening manner with an ax, and question me. I level my boardroom gaze on her and state in a firm tone. "I'll be asking the questions. First off, who the hell are you and what do you think you are doing?" She tightens the grip on her weapon as her eyes move into narrowed slits in a daring glare.

"Look, buddy, I don't know who you think you are, but you don't whip into my drive and start making demands." I lose it and lunge at her to grab the ax, but she is faster than I expected. She lowered it and hit me dead center in the chest with the blunt end, causing me to take a few steps back. I can hear my farm manager's truck starting to come down the drive and am a little perplexed he is just now getting around to noticing this situation. It is his job, after all, to keep an eye on the place.

"Look, lady, I don't know how you people do things across the pond, but here in Scotland, you can't move on to someone else's land, start cutting down their trees, and make a home for yourself. And, you sure as hell can't assault someone with a deadly weapon." I watch in fascination as the tips of her ears turn a brilliant shade of red. In the back of my mind, I remember another little woman whose ears would change a shade right before she would paddle my little behind for talking back. My brother and I knew when mum's ears started to turn red, we better run and hide until the evening meal. Caught up in the memory, I did not notice the blunt end of the ax coming at me again. This time my arse hit the ground and the fierce little woman began to yell as Hamish pulled up to the scene.

"Look, jackass, I DON'T know who YOU think YOU are! I live here, LEE-GAL- LEE!" She says it loud and slow like I am a complete idiot and then continues, "I did not CUT down any trees! What I AM cutting up, was already down, due to storms. Now, I suggest you get your fancy suit up off the ground, crawl back in your POS Rover, take it back down that road, and reassess the tone you take with people when you don't know all the facts."

As I stand, I begin dusting myself off and prepare to go for round two with this little hot-headed beast. Before I can deliver my next argument, Hamish approaches grinning ear to ear. "Declan, you made it back safe...and I see you met Miss Gabriella!" Hamish looks between the two of us, oblivious to the fact the demon woman knocked me to the ground moments ago. Suddenly, awareness lights in his eyes to the tension brewing between me and this little spitfire of a woman. I glance at her taking in her dumbfounded expression at Hamish's words.

She looks to Hamish, "You know this...pompous...arrogant..." she looks me up and down, "overdressed ass."

Hamish's smile falters a bit before he says with a shade of humor in his voice, "Gabriella Fairmont meet Declan Douglas. He owns this estate." Her eyes go the size of saucers, then she narrows her eyes at him. At least I am not the only one who gets this lady's ire now and evidently, Hamish has a lot of explaining to do, to both of us.

"You said you were the owner of this place." She spat out.

Hamish shakes his head, "No, lass, I told you I needed to hire help for the cattle work and the hay."

"Wait a damn minute," I break in, "you mean to tell me you hired a woman, an American woman to work with the livestock and bale the hay?"

Her eyes narrow at me and her ears go a little darker red. "You're the one who hates Americans? Every time someone in town would say they couldn't believe Mr. Douglas hired an American I was confused," her face softens as she looks back at Hamish, "because you and Molly were so nice, welcoming, and made me feel at home." Her features hardened, and her glare falls on me again, "But you, now I understand."

Hamish decides this is the time to sell me on his new employee. Explaining to me with Gabriella's help, they worked all the livestock, the hay was baled and put away. "She was so efficient I think we may bale the east and south fields, leaving the cattle to graze the west until winter hits. When the snow starts to fly, we will move them closer to the barn lot." He turns away from me to face the demon woman, "Actually, Gabriella I came down to talk to you about it. The weatherman is talking rain by Friday, which means Thursday in these parts. If we cut and fluff today, we could bale Monday and do the south field on Tuesday."

I stare at her as she considers. "Aren't the east and south fields combined close to the same acreage as the one we already finished?" Hamish nods and she continues, "Why don't we cut and ted as much as we can today? Monday, as soon as the moisture dries enough, we can bale. Tuesday morning, we can feed and while we wait for the dew to dry, we can haul in the previous days baling. It sounds like more work, but we could be all done by Wednesday night."

Hamish beams at her. "I think that's a clever idea, lass." I can't help but notice she turned her back to me, moving me out of the conversation.

"Let me put the wood splitter up and I will be ready." With the ax in hand, she strolled gracefully to the woodshed, placing her weapon inside. Hamish moved to help her in pushing the splitter back into the building before returning to my side.

I turn to Hamish who is beaming at me. "She is grand, isn't she?"

I look to him disapprovingly, "You know I don't care for Americans, especially American women. They are gold digging untrustworthy creatures that should be nowhere near this property, nor me."

Hamish still smiling like an idiot, states, "she updated the furniture and appliances for the cottage." For the love of all that is holy!

I felt my face take on a hard look of anger, "You let her spend that kind of money on..."

He holds his hand up stopping me mid-sentence. "She purchased all the items herself, with her own funds."

I know shock first registers across my face before my distrusting side moves back in to control, "What is she after?"

Hamish shrugs, "A new life. She even offered to work for free just to live in the cottage."

I look toward the little shack where the woman disappeared inside, "Who is she running from?"

Hamish shakes his head and looks...sad, as his eyes move back to where the woman went in. "It is her story to tell Declan. I will tell you the lass lost her husband and two sons in a car accident. She was the only one who survived. I think she is simply here to get a fresh start. You of all people should understand that."

I grunted in response. If Hamish was implying she and I were anything alike, he fell short of the mark. "I'll see you at supper," I said as I turned to my vehicle. I slid into my Land Rover, but before I drove off I selected a song from my playlist. Childish for a thirty-six-year-old man, maybe, but I am sure I made my point. I rolled down my windows and turned up the volume as, Gabriella, if that is her real name, walks out the door. I drove off as Lenny Kravitz sings, 'American Woman stay away from me.' I wasn't too sure I didn't see her flipping me the bird in my rear-view mirror. Something tightened in my chest and I fought back the amused grin trying to cross my face. This woman would be trouble with a capital "t" and I wanted no part of her nor the problems she brought with her.

Chapter Eight

Declan

Once back home, I settled in my study and find the stack of papers Hamish left on my desk for review. In that pile, I found an employment file for Gabriella Fairmont. Thirty-one-year-old, lives in Missouri, last employed by a long-term care facility, but doesn't say what she did there. Four years of active duty military service and a high school graduate. Though she filled out the application, it held hardly any detailed information, so I do what any good employer would do, turn to the internet. I punch her name into the search bar and find a Facebook account, clicking on it first. Shockingly, unlike the rest of the world, her profile, posts, and pictures were open for the world to see. Her last post says, 'It is going to be hard, but I am picking up the pieces and looking for a change...lookout Scotland, here I come!' I scroll through to find fifty 'happy birthday' wishes she didn't respond to; the date on the messages coincides with what is in her file. A few more scrolls and I found another mass of unanswered birthday regards from the previous year. My eyes then fall on what Hamish mentioned. Lots of, 'sorry for your loss, words cannot even express.' Then a post from a little over a year ago, 'This is Diana, Gabby's sister, mom and I would like to thank you all for your kind words and well wishes. My sister is still unresponsive, but we continue to hope and pray God will wake her soon.' A few scrolls down, ' This is Gabby's Mom, we've decided to go on with funeral arrangements for Daniel and the boys. Gabby's condition hasn't changed. The doctors tell us, even if she did wake up, attending a funeral would be near impossible in her condition'. Scrolling, I find a picture of the woman I met, only with long hair and a little more weight clearly on her face. She is sitting in a vehicle, leaning toward an average looking man with sunglasses on and two young boys peering through the seats behind them. The caption reads, 'Finally going on vacation. First stop, the zoo. Wish us luck.' I click on the photo tab and scroll through several pages of pictures. The woman's entire life is on here. The kids being born, their small wedding, military pics, and birthdays.

I close out of the Facebook, feeling like a voyeur, but decide to search the news reports for any information on her accident. I find it, though I wished I had left it alone. A carload of teens, heading North on a state highway, going thirty miles over the speed limit, decided to pass the car in front of them in a no passing zone on a hill. The report stated the Fairmont's vehicle, driving the posted speed limit and heading southbound, was hit head-on by a northbound vehicle. The four people in the oncoming car were not wearing seatbelts, all pronounced dead at the scene. The impact must have been horrific, all parties in Gabriella's vehicle were wearing safety devices but still died at the scene, except for her. Emergency crew's life-flighted her to an area hospital. A photo of the accident went with the article and made my stomach knot. It looked like the other car merged to become one with the other in a tangle of twisted metal and broken glass. The only part of the entire vehicle that appeared undamaged, the passenger seat, presumably of Gabriella's vehicle.

As I stared at the screen at the image of the damage and the loss, I am pulled back into another accident five years ago, remarkably similar to the one in the picture I was looking at. The difference being the collision occurred with a delivery van and a compact car. I firmly believed it hadn't been an accident at all, though I couldn't prove it. Pouring myself another scotch, I shake off the sadness trying to consume me for this woman and my own memories.

Regardless of who or what she is, she is still an American woman. They say it only takes one bad apple to ruin the bushel. Well, that is exactly what happened to me with Jessica Grant. She was beautiful, tall, and an up and coming model. We met at an annual fundraiser party one of my colleagues hosted. After an hour of conversation, I thought her to be intriguing, smart, witty, and she held a bright future in modeling. Three months in, I find out she lacked the intelligence I thought her to have, as she was addicted to heroin. She had tried to access my bank accounts by forging my signature on my checks and taking them to the very bank which held my accounts. When I attempted to rid myself of her, she played the pregnancy card. She wouldn't provide me with proof, so I manipulated her into believing we were going on a date, picked her up and drove her straight to a well-established rehab clinic. She went ballistic. I informed her if she was having my child, then she was getting help. We walked in and they ordered tests, including a pregnancy test and low and behold, no baby! That had been ten years ago.

Seven years back, I tried again, another American woman, Samantha. We met at a business conference in New York. We went out a few times, which she thought gave her complete control over my life. Every hour she called or texted, sent me pics, some clean, some went straight to the trash. I return to Scotland and a few days later I find her waiting on my front doorstep. She threatened suicide, lawsuits, and tried to ruin my business reputation. The police arrested her and I pressed charges. Two weeks after the arrest, she showed back up at my house with a gun, threatening me, my staff, and anyone who got in her way.

In the midst of all that drama, I met Tess. I found her broken down on the side of the road on my way home from Edinburgh. A sweet, beautiful Scottish woman on her way to stay with family for the summer. In a month's time, I knew she was 'the one'. Tess had been smart, funny, and wanted to remain in the area. Two days after our engagement announcement she left my house, taking her grandmother to see a specialist in Edinburgh. Witnesses say another vehicle forced her into the path of an oncoming delivery van, killing her and her grandmother instantly. The driver of the van was unhurt and the person who caused the accident was never found. Though I couldn't prove it, I knew in my gut who caused the accident. Samantha warned me if anyone got between us they would pay the price. Once the American government returned her to the United States, the FBI promised she would never leave the borders of their country again.

Now, I know I shouldn't throw all American women under the bus for the actions of two, but European women never gave me any trouble whatsoever, however, after the last episode, especially since my gut told me Samantha caused Tess's wreck, I have been leery of all females in general. I found as I get older it is safer and less time consuming to focus on my real estate empire and business dealings rather than trying to please another human being. I shake off thoughts of Jessica, Samantha, Tess, and definitely of Gabriella, returning my attention to my current property acquisition.

Wednesday evening while sitting in my office, I could hear music... loud music. I get up and step out on the second-floor balcony which overlooks the farm. Gabriella is driving a tractor with a bale wagon fully loaded around the barn, followed by Hamish with the loader tractor. I know the tune but can't quite put my finger on it. It is a long shot, but I ask Siri to name the song. 'You're So Vain' by Carly Simon. I pull it up on my computer and listen to the lyrics. I assumed Gabriella just played her card in response to my American Woman throw down earlier in the week. I chuckle as I shake my head and step back into my office. "She has spunk," I say to my screen, before returning to current market projections.

Chapter Nine

Hamish and Molly

Later that night

Getting ready for bed Molly asks Hamish, "What was that all about today?"

"What?" Hamish asks in return.

Molly shakes her head at her husband. "The music? I know Gabriella hasn't been here long, but it seemed to be a bit out of character for her."

Hamish begins to chuckle as he explains, "Two days ago when Declan came back he stopped at the servant's cottage."

"Aye, ye told me about it."

Hamish's lips twitched with a smirk, "What I didn't tell ye, when he pulled away he was blaring that American Woman song." Molly tisks and shakes her head as Hamish continues. "I told ye she whacked him with the ax?"

"Aye, ye did, but what does that have to do with anything?"

"Instead of fighting her with fists or words, he hit back with a song. I'd say today, she gave it back to him. Kind of funny if ye ask me."

Molly harrumphed in indignation, "Well, it sounds like grade school childish behavior if ye ask me. I can't imagine Declan acting so immature."

"I tell ye Molly, when I walked up on them staring each other down, I couldn't tell if they were going to duke it out or kiss it out. The tension was so thick between the two of them ye couldn't have cut it with Gabby's ax."

Molly huffed, "Well, I won't have it. They both bein' old enough to act like civil grownups."

Hamish shakes his head at his wife, "Oh let it alone Molly. Declan is leaving on Monday for another two-week conference in New York."

"Again? He just got back."

"Maybe he is seeing someone there."

Molly snorts "Aye and I will sprout wings and fly off to the fae kingdom tomorrow."

Chapter Ten

Gabriella

Thursday morning, I awoke to the sound of my phone ringing. I fumble a bit before picking it up from the nightstand, looking bleary-eyed at the time first, four thirty and then the caller. With full on croaky morning voice, I rasped out, "Hello, Hamish. Is something wrong?"

I hear a slight chuckle on the other end of the line, "Sorry lass. Did I wake ye?"

I wanted to answer, um, it is four thirty in the dang morning. Instead, I gave him a cheery, "Yeah, but it's okay. What can I do for you Hamish?"

"Sorry lass, but I need your help. We've gotta cow having trouble calving and I could use an extra set of hands."

"I'll be there in ten minutes." I hung up and got out of bed heading for the bathroom. After using the facilities, I washed my hands and brushed my teeth. I decided to forgo the hair as I tied a bandanna over my head. Dashing into my bedroom, I pulled open drawers, taking out a pair of jeans, a long sleeve thermal shirt, and socks. As I shoved my feet into my boots, I opened the door and a rain storm greeted me. Scratch that, a torrential downpour of epic proportions was taking place outside. I stepped back into the house grabbed a hoodie and a rain slicker. I slipped off my everyday boots in exchange for my Mucks before heading out the door, I wasted no time getting into the truck.

I pulled around to the barn, jumped out and made a mad dash to the doors. Before I entered, I caught sight of Hamish in the feedlot, kneeling in the mud. Trudging through the muddy slosh, I went to his side. "I tried to get her into the barn, but this was as far as she made it before going down." I knelt next to the cow and we began the tiring process of trying to pull the calf from the mother. After thirty minutes of no progress Hamish looks at me with grief-stricken eyes, "I'm afraid this is a lost cause. She's exhausted and the baby is wedged." Without saying a word, I knelt beside him and ran my hands along the cow's belly. I could feel her contracting and the calf moving. Walking on my knees in the mud and muck, I moved to the backside of the cow. Using the knowledge gained from my father and my nursing skills, I reached into the canal and felt for the baby's head. Reaching in a little further I feel the calf. He twisted just enough to make it near impossible for him to slip on out as he should.

I looked back to Hamish, "When I tell you to, pull." He nodded. I worked on moving the calf into position and waited for the next contraction. When it came, I yelled, "Pull now Hamish!"

By six a.m. the rain had soaked me to the bone and I trembled with cold. Hamish patted my shoulder and said, "Go see if Molly has coffee and breakfast, I'll be right in."

I smiled wearily at him, "You had me at coffee." I walked into the mudroom off the kitchen and removed my boots. I made quick work of rolling up the legs of my jeans, so I would minimize the wet muck tracking on the floor.

"Oh, you poor dear. Did Hamish have you out in this storm?" Molly came at me, dish towel in hand as if she were going to pat me down.

"He did. If you have some coffee on, I would greatly appreciate a cup." I heard a snicker to my left and tensed seeing Declan sitting at the little breakfast table in the corner reading a newspaper. "Something in there amusing you?" I asked snidely.

"No... the stench of the barn lot muck coming from you caused me to catch my breath for a moment."

I stared at him disbelieving and opened my mouth to tell him he should like the smell of his own kind; however, Molly beat me to it. "Declan..." She exhaled in annoyance, "that'll be enough." He shot Molly an apologetic glance which I would have missed if I wasn't staring daggers at the arrogant ass. Molly handed me the steaming cup of coffee.

I turned to Declan and said, "Well, at least I was here for Hamish to call. I would hate for you to get your Armani suit or Gucci shoes dirty. Although with your head so far up your own ass, at least you would have known what end to work with." And before he or Molly could say a word I walked back into the mudroom, put on my boots, and headed for the barn. I passed Hamish on his way in.

"Is something wrong Lass?"

I handed him my full untouched mug of coffee. "Nope, just thought I'd get a jump on the chores." Tears were threatening to fall, and I wanted to be alone before they made their escape.

Hamish stared at me like he wanted to press further, but he let it go. He explained he had headed out early in an attempt to beat the storm, which led him to finding the cow having trouble. "I had planned to call you at six thirty and tell you not to worry about coming in due to the rain."

For the first time since arriving here, relief filled me to be off for the day. "Okay, Hamish. If you need anything else, don't hesitate to give me a call." He waved me off and I headed for the truck.

Once I found solace and safety in my little cottage, I burst into tears and slumped to the floor. Honest to God I didn't know why my emotions got the better of me. After the trying time with the cow or the complete negativity of the arrogant Mr. Douglas, I had no clue, but one of the two led me to this breakdown. Both incidents replayed in my mind. I give myself a few minutes of self-pity before I picked myself up off the floor. I went to the kitchen to start my own pot of coffee then headed to the shower.

Chapter Eleven

Declan

Hamish stormed into the kitchen, "What in the name of all the saints did ye do to that poor girl?" Molly stood at the stove turning a ham steak shaking her head but kept silent. I lay my newspaper down and looked at him over the rim of my mug of coffee, taking a drink. "Well, is someone going to answer me? She looked like someone shot her prized foxhound. "He looked at Molly, who remained quiet. Then he leveled his gaze on me. "Declan. I've known ye dang near your whole life and for the life of me, I cannot understand why ye would treat Gabby with such disdain. She answered my call at four thirty in the God blessed morning and was arrived within fifteen minutes. She worked with me in the middle of a downpour to save one of your cows. I was at a complete loss without her. Matter of fact, I was ready to give up and get the gun. But not Gabriella, no sir. She moved in, took control of the situation and manipulated the calf internally. When I sent her in here, she was exhausted but proud of the work she did, as she should have been. A few minutes later she looked defeated."

I knew if I didn't speak up the old man would continue, so I spoke, "I might've indicated she, um, smelled like the barnyard." Well, saying it out loud made me sound like the royal arse I'd acted like. "But, in my defense, she did call me a jackass with my head up my backside."

Molly decided to speak up, "After ye told her the stench of the barnyard caused ye to choke up." Hamish leveled his glare on me. Yes, this is my estate and he my foreman, however, the man was like a second father to me so rather than be angry with him, I took my scolding like a man.

"Declan, I suggest ye take yourself down the road and apologize to Gabriella." He gritted out through clenched teeth. My face must have showed pure panic, because Hamish continued, "Look, ye don't need to be her friend. Ye don't have to like the lass at all, but ye need to at least give her the same respect ye would expect and give to any other employee." I grumbled in defeat, finished my coffee and headed for the door.

I knock on the cottage front door three times, but she didn't answer. For some unexplained reasoning in my brain, I begin to panic wondering if something happened to her. I walk around to the back door surprised to find it unlocked. I slip inside and call out her name. No answer, but I could hear the shower running. I should leave and come back later. Again, my brain decides we are going to sit down and drink a cup of coffee. I poured a mug of the fresh brew, sat down at the little kitchenette, and check out the new appliances she had bought. I noted what she had bought wasn't outlandish or top of the line, but functional. I make a mental note to call McLeay's to find out what she spent so I could reimburse her when she leaves. There was no way she wouldn't be taking these items with her when she goes back home.

Lost in my thoughts, I did not hear the shower shut off and was a little surprised when the current bane of my existence strolled into the kitchen in nothing but a towel. She, in her own world, oblivious to me sitting at the table, walked straight to the coffee pot, took down a mug, and filled it. She turned, seen me sitting at the table and all hell broke loose. Time slowed, I sat still as a statue as she let out an ear-piercing scream, dropped the steaming cup of coffee, and of course, at that precise moment her towel came undone. Everything hit the floor. Glass shards flew in all directions and dark hot liquid splattered around her feet and ankles. I watched as recognition dawned on her face and quickly changed to pure anger if the reddening of her ears was any indication. She screamed, "WHAT IN THE EVER-LOVING HELL ARE YOU DOING IN HERE?"

Time went from standing still, to fast forward as I jumped up from my seat. Without saying a word, I grabbed her towel, shook it a bit, wrapped it around her, and plucked her up from where she stood. Turning, I took two strides toward the living room before sitting her back down. Her eyes were huge as I stammered, "Glass, floor, didn't want you...cut your feet." Holy hell, I couldn't even speak in complete sentences. "Go, put something on, I will clean this up."

Her eyes narrowed, and her ears turned red, " You will get the heck out of my cottage you...you...freaking perv. Oh my God! It wasn't enough for you to make your snarky comments an hour ago, you had to come down here and dish out some more? GET OUT!" She walked to the bedroom and slammed the door.

I turned back to the kitchen at a complete loss as to what I should do. She wanted me gone and I should respect her wishes, however, this situation was indeed my doing, so I swept up all the shattered glass pieces I could see, wiped up the splattered coffee, and left the way I came in. At least I could tell Hamish, I tried to apologize.

Chapter Twelve

Gabriella

I stood in the center of my bedroom replaying the last few minutes in my head. My eyes closed in complete and utter mortification when the memory of standing before Declan Douglas, bare naked, replayed through my mental picture show. No one, not a soul, had seen my skin since I left the hospital. The jagged scar running diagonally from my right shoulder to my left hip wasn't as bad as it had been in the beginning, however someone looking couldn't miss the raised darkened scarring that stood out against my pale skin. That...that Neanderthal sat there and stared at me like a museum exhibit! Well, until he decided to manhandle me out of the kitchen!

I had no earthly idea what he was doing in my house. The arrogant pig went stupid, losing his ability to speak and I lost my cool. Well, who could blame me? As my anger began to subside the stinging pain in my feet grabbed my attention. I looked down to the reddened skin. No doubt from the scalding hot coffee I managed to splatter all over myself in my agitation of seeing a strange man, who wasn't supposed to be in my house. Who in the blue blazes just goes into someone else's space, unannounced, and make themselves at home? Declan Douglas, that is the kind of person to do something like that!

I shook off my anger and dressed. Upon returning to the kitchen I sighed in relief to find the room empty, though he did sweep up the broken glass and tried to wipe up the spilled coffee before leaving. The lone cup still sitting on the table where he had left it, the only evidence the events actually happened. I poured myself another mug and sat down across from where he had been. For several minutes, I stared at his mug before I decided to call my sister. Whatever Declan Douglas wanted wasn't important enough to waste any more of my energy on. As I grabbed my phone I stopped, realizing it was about two in the morning back home. I would have to wait to talk to her, so I sent her a text to call me when she had time.

∞ ∞ ∞

As the torrential downpour slowed to a steady light rain, I finished my lunch and with nothing to do on the farm, decided it would be a good time to explore the property. I called Hamish up to ask if he minded if I took the side by side out for a drive. He said it'd be okay, but I felt he wanted to say more to me. "Hamish, is everything all right?"

He hesitated for a beat, "Aye lass, all is well."

"How are the calf and cow doing?" I couldn't help but shake the feeling he was upset with the events of the morning, but for the life of me I couldn't figure out why he would be angry with me.

"They are getting along well. Listen, about Declan..." He began, but I cut him off.

"Hamish, you are not responsible for Declan. He is a grown man, who obviously has a problem with me, but that is his problem. Not yours and certainly not mine. I enjoy working for you and with you. I will do my best to stay out of his way."

Hamish let out a heavy sigh, "I enjoy working with you to lass, you remind me of my own daughter. I will try to keep our work out of the line of Declan's wrath, but sooner rather than later he is going to have to learn to play nice."

I giggled to myself knowing Declan was going to be punished like a first grader, "Well, it sounds like a plan. I will see you in the morning, Hamish."

"Kay, lass, be careful out there." Once I hung up I headed for my truck to go retrieve the side by side.

I made a trek out through the pastures to a wooded area to where I believed the perimeter of the property lay. The rain slowed to a fine, steady drizzle, so I left the ATV and began to explore on foot. Birds were beginning to chirp happy little tones and rabbits playfully hopped along the forest floor. As I walked through the trees I let my fingers lightly graze over the rain dampened leaves on the lower branches. Taking in the glorious views and sounds around me, an overwhelming sense of peace filled me. I didn't have any clue as to how far I had walked, but soon I found myself moving out of the forest and into a large clearing. As I kept walking I noticed the area was the shape of an almost perfect circle and dead center of that circle was an enormous rounded white rock. Looking it over, I could see nothing special about the stone, just an ordinary rock in the middle of a field. I couldn't help myself, I climbed on top of it, raised my hands into the air and called out, "I call upon the circle stones and the fae queen, to fulfill my dreams and bring me to happy." I sat down on the cool firm surface and chuckled. I couldn't wait to tell Diana, I had found a circle stone to make my wish on.

I sat there for a while until the sun started to kiss the tops of the trees on its descent into the western sky. As I stood, my eyes moved to the opposite side of the clearing from where I entered. There in the shadows of the trees, I caught a flash of red. As I stared at the object a form began to take shape. A woman in a red cloak edged a few steps out of the shadows making her more visible, a redheaded woman watching me through...was that...a rifle? "Holy Mary..." I started to yell but cut my sentence short when I heard the shot ring out. Without thinking, I launched myself off the rock and ran. I made it to the trees and didn't look back. I ran as fast and as hard as I could, branches smacking me in the face and catching in my hair, but I kept running. When I broke through the trees where I thought the ATV should be, I paused a second in alarm, nothing sat there! In a panic and feeling the need to get away, I began turning in all directions. As I did, I scanned the ground looking for the tracks where I drove into the field. In the grass I could see faint tire impressions but no side by side in sight. Another shot rang through the air, making a whistling sound near my head. The roof of the main house glistened as a single beam of sunlight punctured through the clouds making it my beacon to guide me to safety. I dashed across the field like my life depended on it, given someone was shooting at me, it did.

My lungs started to burn, and my legs were throbbing, but I pushed through the pain; I needed to reach the safety of the house. As I neared the perimeter of the yard, I caught sight of Hamish as he came around the corner of the barn, looking around in confusion. I watched in growing alarm as Molly stepped out of the backdoor calling something to Hamish. I waved frantically with my hand screaming, "Inside, inside, gun, inside." They watched as if a lunatic were on the loose. Then another shot rang through the air and their eyes went wide with horror. Within a split second of hearing the sound, I threw myself to the ground sliding through the mud left after the morning's rainstorm.

Rolling to my back I lifted my head to look back in the direction I ran from but saw nothing. "Molly, call the constable's office" I heard Hamish yell.

I heard Declan's commanding voice, "For the love of God, what is going on out here?" Simultaneously another shot fired, hitting the ground an inch away from my hip, where I lay sprawled out. In a swift, but jerky movement, I rolled to my stomach, pushed to my feet, and ran inside the house, followed by a worried Hamish and a fierce, red-faced Declan.

It took me a solid three minutes to get my breathing under control before I could answer questions. I told them my location, the woman I seen, the side by side gone and they pretty much knew the rest. Declan looked for a change, troubled and concerned about my explanation. "Are you sure you were at the circled clearing?"

"Yes." I declared, pointing through the window toward the field. "I drove the ATV out there until I came to the tree line. I walked through the woods until I found the clearing." I left the part out about my wish and spinning on the stone. "I thought I was still on your property. I didn't know your neighbors were crazy!" I said halfheartedly. Declan turned confused, angry eyes in my direction, "They aren't! This property runs clear to the ocean on that side. If you would have continued west, you would have come to the cliffs. No one should be out there at all."

I shook my head, "Well, somebody is out there, and she is not happy."

Within thirty minutes the local police arrived, and I gave my statement. I noticed they were eyeing Declan with suspicion. Surely, they didn't think he did this, did they? Declan spoke to them with a surly demeanor before he, Hamish, and the officers headed for the door to search the area for the missing ATV. As they were exiting the house Molly handed me a hot cup of peppermint tea and ushered me into a bathroom to clean up. A quick look in the mirror and I gaped in shock. I looked like I had been rolling around on the forest floor. Smudges of mud coated my face like a three-year-old had painted me up. Tiny scratches, some slightly bleeding, others reddened, intermixed with the mud. Leaves and twigs sporadically stuck out in all directions from my hair. If I didn't know any better, I would've thought I was the crazy woman. Deciding the damage was worse than I expected, I turned on the shower and removed my nasty clothes trying to place them in a pile that would not leave a huge mess.

A few minutes after stepping under the warm spray, I heard a light tapping on the door and the click of it opening. "It's Molly lass. I brought ye some clean clothes to change into. I will take your clothes down and put them in the wash."

"Thanks Molly. I will be down in a few." The soft click as the door latched, her only response.

After my shower, I stood staring at the clothing Molly left for me, shaking my head. I had two options, go out in a towel, or put the cursed things on. Well, I guess there was a third choice. I could go streaking, butt naked out the front door and make a beeline for my cottage. Nope, that wasn't going to happen. I faced the situation and put on the clothes. With no plausible explanation, my skin began to tingle as I pulled the four sizes too big shirt over my head. It hit me at knee-level on my five-foot two stature. Grabbing the plaid flannel pajama pants, I was surprised to find they weren't too big in the waist but did fall about two yards too long. Daniel had not been a big man, just a few inches separated us in height, so his clothing usually fit nicely on my small build. Declan's clothing, him being at least a foot taller than me and very muscular, were several sizes too big. The shirt alone fell over me like an unfitted tee shirt dress.

I made my way back to the kitchen, where Molly sat me down and began to pat ointment on the scratches on my face. "I never noticed this before." She whispered to me.

"What?" I knew what she saw, but didn't want to talk about it

"This scar on your forehead." She grazed her finger delicately across it as she moved my damp hair. Her eyes followed the distinct line to the top of my head.

"When my hair is dry and down, it isn't noticeable, unless you are up close and looking for it. Most of the time it is covered by the bandanna I wear." I explained in a soft whisper. Originally, the gash ran from the top of my right eyebrow and straight back into my hairline. I felt fortunate the scarring didn't start until further up my forehead and most people were never close enough to my face to see it.

Molly started to ask another question when the back door opened, an angry faced Declan stomped in with Hamish following him. I stood in such a rush my chair teetered on its legs, "Did you find anything?" He stopped dead in his tracks and looked me up, down, and up again. The anger left his face and a flicker of...amusement, crossed his features before he schooled it into a mask of indifference. "We found the ATV," Hamish spoke with a disgusted sound to his voice.

"I am going to call the insurance company." Declan gave no further explanation and stomped out of the room and up the stairs.

I looked to Hamish, who rubbed a weary hand through his hair. "We followed the tracks to where you indicated you stopped. We could even see the footpath and prints where you went in and came out. We trailed more tire prints from where it had been moved...to out by the cliffs."

He said no more on the matter. Molly piped up, "Well, if you found it, why is Declan having to call the insurance company?"

Hamish took a seat and lowered his head. "Because whoever took it spray painted 'Die Whore! He is mine!' down both sides in red paint, then poised it to be shoved off the cliff edge." Molly sharply took in a breath in horror.

I sat down. Someone wanted me dead, because of Declan? "That doesn't make any sense. Why would someone, a woman, find me to be a threat? Clearly, anyone who knows Declan knows he doesn't like Americans not to mention I have no interest in him."

Hamish shook his head, "Doesn't matter. If it is who he thinks it is, well, let me just say the woman doesn't have all her chickens in one coop."

Molly crossed herself, "Lord, I hope that woman isn't back. Gabriella, why don't you stay here in the main house for a few days, until they catch her and remove her from the country?"

"No, it won't be necessary, I'll make sure the doors and windows are locked tight at all times. I will be fine." I declared, though I felt unsure about the statement, but sleeping under the same roof as Declan Douglas, simply couldn't happen, crazy woman or not.

"She is right." A voice comes from the other room as Declan made his way back into the kitchen. "You will be safer here at the main house than at your home. This is not the first time Samantha's level of crazy has been a problem. Once it is in her head you're a problem or in her way, she will stop at nothing to get rid of you, trust me on that. The police are coming back tomorrow morning to do a full sweep of the property and they ensured me an all-points bulletin was sent out for a crazy American woman." He smirked teasingly at me with his last statement.

Now, pieces of the puzzle were coming together, "She is the reason you are against American women?" His brows drew together, and he nodded a little self-deprecating. "Well, I can certainly understand your distaste now." I continued a little chuckle in my voice. And I could. He looked to me with shock in his eyes that I would understand. "I will stay for a few days or until they catch her if it will make you feel better."

"Hamish will escort you down to get some of your things and Molly will ready a room for you." He gave a single nod to each of them having given his orders and left the room.

Chapter Thirteen

Declan

I put a call into my assistant Tim, explaining to him the latest Samantha situation here at the estate. He would reschedule my next conference to make it a live video feed. I gave him the details of what occurred. I concluded with an explanation of not being comfortable leaving Hamish and Molly to fend for themselves. I also explained to him a new employee moved in and didn't know of the earlier debacle and that she is the latest focus of Samantha's ire. He assured me he would handle the particulars and rang off to take care of business.

I poured two fingers of whiskey and sat back in my chair. According to the agent that dealt with my case the last time, if Miss Davis ever managed to leave the United States again, he would personally call to notify me. Someone dropped the ball and almost cost a woman her life. Stewing on that a moment, I picked up the phone and dialed a number I hoped I would never need to call again. "Agent Ferguson." He answered after three rings.

"Agent Ferguson. Declan Douglas."

A brief pause, "Mr. Douglas, it's been a while."

His tone betrayed him, I could hear the confusion he tried to cover. The fact he was the lead agent on the U.S. side of my problem, I felt he should know exactly why I was calling. "Tell me, Agent..." I spat out the agent like it was a bitter taste in my mouth, "where is Samantha Davis?" Silence, then I could hear tapping on the keys of a computer keyboard. "Let me tell you." I decided to spare him the search. "She is somewhere near or on my property in Scotland. I know this because she shot off at least four rounds at my newest employee. To top it off, she stole an ATV that said employee drove out to a clearing, spray painted 'Die Whore, he is mine' down both sides and left it ready to be shoved off a cliff. I assume with said employee's body inside. Now, Agent, would you like to explain to me how any of this was possible. Samantha Davis is supposed to be on every government watch list on the globe. She should have had zero possibility of even leaving the United States."

He hesitated, "I have no idea. Are you sure it was her?"

Well, that took me aback a little. Mainly, because considering the situation, no I wasn't positive at all, but in all truthfulness, it couldn't be anyone else. "I cannot say I am a hundred percent sure it was her. I can tell you, my employee's description of what she saw, fit Samantha to a tee. However, the employee was also running for her life."

"I will check in to it Declan and call you back." He assured

"I would appreciate it." I spat out before slamming down the phone.

My next call went to Wentworth Security. The house security system could use an update and I might even consider upgrading to perimeter security as well. Within ten minutes, they scheduled to do an update and perimeter quote first thing in the morning. I also order four quick response pendants for the staff and myself. I refused to take chances with my life or the lives of my employees. Samantha or not, I wouldn't rest knowing my family was in any danger. Family? What an odd thought. Sure, Hamish and Molly were like family to me, but Gabriella? Well, she was another headache I didn't need; however I couldn't help the overwhelming feeling deep in my gut I needed to protect her.

I decided to eat my supper in my office avoiding any confrontations with the woman downstairs. Of course, I held a slight fear that she might bring up the incident at the cottage this morning. I managed to avoid Hamish and Molly when I returned home from Gabriella's house. This afternoon and evening's events didn't leave time for a conversation about what occurred. No sense in tempting the wrath of any person downstairs after the day we had.

As I tossed and turned in my bed trying to sleep, images of Gabriella standing in the kitchen in my clothes kept playing over in my head. Her damp hair combed back, the light scar on her forehead moving back into her hairline. That image morphed into mental pictures of her standing naked in her own kitchen, bared to me. My mind registered the scar running across her torso, but I found it insignificant. My focus fell on her beauty as a woman. I had been with my fair share of women in my twenties. Not so much since I turned thirty. I was interested in women, I just wanted more and couldn't find the right one.

Gabriella fell far from the right one but seeing her standing there...God...I couldn't explain the emotions coming over me. All I could think, my only concern at the time, I didn't want her to cut her pretty little feet on the glass. Hell, I even found her feet to be pretty. Before I knew it, my brain shut down and my body took over. Getting out of the chair and physically moving her out of harm's way of its own accord. But, alas, I swore off American women, not to mention she worked for me. Gabriella Fairmont was off limits in every way with a big red

'restricted' stamped across her beautiful face.

∞ ∞ ∞

Three days later, sitting in my office going over a purchase contract for a Las Vegas hotel, a loud pitched pinging noise caught my attention. Half a second later my cell phone lit up with a text alert: WEST DOOR, UNAUTHORIZED ACCESS. No one ever used that door. I bolted out of my chair and retrieved the nine-millimeter Beretta I stashed in the top right drawer of my desk. A split second later my cell phone rang. I snatched it up before the first ring ended, "Douglas."

"Mr. Douglas, this is Tyler with Wentworth Security. We have an alert you have an intruder in the home. We have contacted the local authorities and they are on their way. Are you or anyone else in immediate danger?" Tyler was very calm and collected.

I, however, was not. "Tyler, I have no idea. I am on the second floor. At present, it's myself and one other person on the property today, but I do not have eyes on her." I was going to continue when I heard a woman screech from the stairwell, "You whore!" Then a familiar voice, "Not on my watch honey!" followed by a thud. I dropped the phone on my desk, opened my office door and did a quick peek around the frame. My mouth fell open as I stood there, stupefied. Samantha lay sprawled out unconscious on the floor, Gabriella standing over her with Hamish's walking stick held like a baseball bat. Two heartbeats later, four uniformed police officers and two suits came bursting through the front door guns raised and pointing at Gabriella.

Chapter Fourteen

Gabriella

I enjoyed staying in the main house for the most part. Every morning Molly served coffee and breakfast after the first run of chores. She even washed my clothes, though I told her I could wash my own clothing. She insisted it was no problem to add in one more of everything to the wash, so I let it go. My biggest issue, I couldn't seem to get a restful night sleep. The room itself and the bed were super comfy, with lots of pillows and warm blankets. The man, rather thoughts of the man, two doors down made falling asleep difficult. I avoided him as much as possible and he avoided me as well, but every time I did sleep I would dream of his face. His emerald green eyes looking at me, not with anger, but with love. His square jaw, with dark scruff that my fingers would lightly touch. He would reach his hand out to me and say something I couldn't hear. Then I would wake up. For two nights I woke up wondering what he said to me.

On the third day, after I finished cleaning out the stalls for winter calving I would ask Hamish if I could go to the cottage and take a nap. Maybe, I could sleep without dreaming there, at least I hoped. Taking a break from cleaning the second stall, I head for the house to get a drink, when I caught sight of a red-headed woman sneaking around the side of the structure. I left my phone in the truck, so I couldn't call anyone. Hamish and Molly went into town for a supply and grocery run, so they weren't in any danger, but Declan was in the house, presumably in his office. Quickly I tapped the pendent Declan insisted we all wear after the previous incident. Outside the back door I could see Hamish's oak walking stick he used when moving cattle, along with the hotshot we used to goose the livestock into the shoot. Odd for Hamish to leave it sitting there, but definitely to my benefit.

Peeking through the back windows of the mudroom, I could see the redhead Declan called Samantha, going toward the staircase. Without a sound, I opened the door and slid quietly inside, making sure to sidestep the squeaky board just inside the door. I didn't pause to take my boots off, I kept moving. I made it to the wall the staircase went up behind. I whipped around to see her on the fourth step up. I reached out with the hot shot, sending a jolt of electric shock into her thigh. She turned on me screaming, "You whore!" Before she could utter another word, I hit her upside the head with the walking stick. She went down like a sack of potatoes and tumbled the four steps to the bottom of the staircase. Hearing a noise, I looked up to see Declan at the top of the stairs, gun in hand, mouth wide open in shock, or horror, I couldn't tell.

Suddenly a rush of sound and movement came from behind me. I whirled, stick held like a ball bat, to find four uniformed officers and two guys who looked like they stepped off the set of MIB running in the front door guns drawn and aimed right at me. I dropped my stick and put my hands up.

"She's good, she's with me." I heard Declan say firmly, as one of the officers began to pat me down, while the other two men held their weapons trained on me. The other two with guns aimed at the crazy woman on the floor.

"I don't think I killed her, but I hit her pretty hard." I said with a note of panic in my voice. Each of the four men looked to each other before looking back at me confusion etched on their faces. "You're an American?" One of the suits asked and then glanced at Declan.

"I am American, but I am not the crazy American." I tilted my head to who I assume was Samantha. "She is the one who shot at me." Eyes never leaving the man in the suit I remarked, "You're American too." He stared at me a second, bemused by the brash tone of my statement. In my defense I was coming down from an adrenaline high and my brain was starting to shut down. Pleasantness was off the table at this point.

"Do you have ID?" The one who appeared to be in charge nearly demanded.

Before I could answer Declan cut in, "I assure you, she is with me agent."

The agent narrowed his eyes at Declan, "She might be Mr. Douglas, but you also said she was new." Great! Like, the arrogant ass already didn't like me, let's add suspicion to his lists of why he doesn't like me. "Again, ma'am, do you have ID?"

"In my back pocket." I never went anywhere without some form of ID on me, you never knew what might happen. My present situation included.

The officer who patted me down started forward, but Declan stopped him. "Do not touch her again. I will get it." What in the world was wrong with him? He sounded, well, he sounded like it bothered him for the man who was simply doing his job, to touch me. I felt him place a soft warm hand on my shoulder. "Which pocket Gab?" He asked, warm breath tickling the back of my neck and my heart skipped a beat as he shortened my name. No one, not even Daniel had ever called me, Gab.

"Right back pocket," I spoke in a whisper as a shiver ran through me. I felt the tips of his fingers as they retrieved the small card from my back pocket. He handed my ID to the agent, who left the house in quick strides. Declan kept his hand on my shoulder while two of the officers searched the downed woman for weapons, finding a fully loaded revolver and a knife.

The suit returned a few minutes later announcing, "Lieutenant Colonel Fairmont, my apologies. We just wanted to make sure Mr. Douglas was one hundred percent covered this time." I took my ID back from him and moved to help Molly, who bustled in from the kitchen with a tray of freshly brewed coffee and mugs . She and Hamish returned as the police were moving into the house. Agent Ferguson ran my identification through whatever computer program he had in his car. Of course, he came back with a resounding, ' not crazy' American woman, with authorization to be in the country. I didn't miss the questioning quirk of Declan's brow when the agent addressed me by my rank. I gave him a nonchalant shrug as I moved away from his hand, still placed on my shoulder. The two uniformed officers took Samantha away while agents Ferguson and Jackson remained behind to explain how she managed to get out of the US and into Scotland.

Samantha stole her comatose sister's identity to get out of the country. Younger by two years and an unflagged travel file due to her vegetative state the past fifteen years following a car accident in her teens. The FBI felt no need to flag her travel files, even though every other person related to Samantha had been.

I slipped into a little crazy American upon hearing they dropped the ball. "Your oversight in this matter came too close to costing all of us our lives."

He nodded in resignation. "I apologize, and I would like to request for you to press attempted murder charges on her to ensure she is locked up this time. Declan, you will also need to file another charge of breaking and entering."

Declan gruffly replied, "I will do whatever needs to be done to keep that woman from stepping foot near us again." Agent Ferguson made a move for his laptop to start filing the necessary paperwork.

Chapter Fifteen

Gabriella

September and October went by without much drama or major problems. Monday through Saturday Hamish and I worked, weaned, and sorted cattle. We went through birth records to determine which cows continued to profit the Douglas estate and made note of the ones which would need to go to market. I sent Agent Ferguson a signed and notarized statement of facts of the attempted murder Samantha endeavored to act out, so I didn't need to fly back to the US for court. Declan, on the other hand, simply extended his business trip for a hotel purchase in Las Vegas. He would be present at the hearing and give his statement of events.

Late in October Hamish and I loaded a trailer of cattle to take to market. On most trips to the sale barn I rode along with him, taking the opportunity to get off the estate for a couple hours. However, as I headed for the passenger door, he stopped me. "Gabby, don't know if you are aware or not, but the weather reports coming through are calling for an unseasonably bad winter storm to hit over the weekend."

"Yes, Hamish. Since the weather started turning colder I check it regularly."

He nodded his head as if he were surprised but proud I thought to check it often. "Instead of riding along today, I would like for you to pack a few items and come to the house. We could be without power for days and if it hits like they are saying, we won't be getting out for a few days either." Declan was gone, but stil, I really didn't want to go to the big house. I really enjoyed the solace of my little cottage. Hamish must've read my mind because he cleared his throat, "Or you could go into town and stock up on supplies. Check with Molly on the things she keeps stocked up."

I nodded giving him the answer, but added, "What about the chores? Won't you need help?"

Hamish shook his head, "All I'll be doing is feeding hay and putting the cows getting ready to calve in the barn stalls. Everything is under control and for the most part, the position I hired you for ended a few days ago. I agreed you could stay till spring, I hope you stay for next season, but will understand if you decide to return home."

I knew when he hired me, he only needed help with the hay and moving cattle around. "Hamish, I know our agreement, but if you need me, you call me."

"Aye lass. I will, but for now, let's get you through your first winter in Scotland."

I decided to take Hamish's advice and find out what items Molly considered a must have for winter survival here. As Hamish drove down the drive, I headed into the house. An hour and a cup of coffee later, I headed into town. Scotland winter didn't sound much different than a few of the storms we suffered through growing up, so I wasn't completely ignorant to the list Molly gave me. I figured I would do grocery shopping and stack some wood inside the mudroom porch of my cottage this afternoon.

∞ ∞ ∞

By Friday evening, I could hear the fierce wind and freezing rain starting to pelt my small cottage windows. Even though he didn't need me to, I helped Hamish finish up the cattle chores before lunch, giving me the rest of the day to bring in more firewood. I stacked up wood everywhere, the mudroom, next to the stove, and some on the front porch. If I could avoid going out into that mess, I would. By eight o'clock Friday night, exhaustion set in and I decided an early night was just what I needed. As I crawled into bed thoughts of Declan popped into my mind. He would return Monday evening and I hoped he made it back safely. I hated the thought of him driving home in these kinds of conditions, hopefully the roads would still be clear providing him safe passage.

I shook thoughts of Declan Douglas away. I shouldn't be thinking of him, not to mention he was not my concern at all. Since the incident with Samantha, he acted a bit more cordial toward me, but I still felt he would prefer it if I left the estate. I liked being here except for him. Shaking the man from my thoughts, I wondered if I should consider going back home in the spring. I fell asleep running through my mind the pros and cons of staying in Scotland.

Chapter Sixteen

Declan

My flight into Edinburgh was the last one allowed to land at the airport. Delayed travelers trying to get to their destination packed the place from wall to wall, making it difficult to maneuver to the exits. I don't recall ever being so thankful to make it back to Scotland. Now, to get to the long-term parking and my SUV and home before the roads iced over.

Most everyone had retired to the safety of their home, as there were few cars on the usually packed city streets. I passed a few drunkards walking along the sidewalks going from one pub to the next, however the further out I traveled from Edinburgh the icier the conditions became and the fewer autos I met on the road. I made it into Dochas and considered stopping at Agnes's B&B, but I could be home in an hour if I took it slow. I switched over to four-wheel drive and left town. About two miles from my estate, something jumped out in front of my Rover. I automatically responded by jerking the wheel to avoid contact. Unfortunately, that action caused me to spin out of control and into the ditch where my vehicle jolted to a loud, crunching stop by colliding with a large old oak tree. Stunned, I sat still for several minutes doing a mental evaluation. Finding no injuries. I glance at my watch which read six-thirty-seven. From the view of the driver's seat I could see the front end of the Rover and knew it wasn't getting out. I bundled up the best I could and stepped out into the icy freezing mix of rain and snow for a long walk. If I could at least make it to the cottage, I would be alright. Gabriella wouldn't turn me away in this weather I hoped. I turned on my phone's flashlight app and began the two-mile trek.

I walked for what seemed like hours, noting the trek was becoming more difficult the further I went. Glancing at my phone screen I found it had only been about an hour and a half. The walk became more difficult with each step as the coldness began to move into my body and the snowfall became heavier. My entire body went numb with the cold. My lips felt frozen shut and my eyes froze wide open. I prayed to God the cottage was close. A scant distance ahead and I could see the large boulder which stood along the edge of the drive. A normally pleasing sight, I found it discouraging as it meant the distance to warmth would be further than I thought. The large rock marked the halfway point from the end of the road to my house and Gabriella's house sat about halfway between the two. I stopped to rest for a moment and looked at my phone screen. No service and the battery had 4% left. I took in a deep breath and forced myself to get up to start walking again. If I stayed out here much longer I would die or at the very least lose my toes. No one at the estate knew about me coming home early and Tim wouldn't question my lack of communication until mid-morning.

I made it a bit further up the drive and glanced down at my phone to see the time, ten thirty-five. When I took off walking, I knew I could make it to Gabriella's, not so much now. I began imagining Hamish finding my frozen, dead corpse in the middle of the driveway in a few days. My world plunged into complete darkness as my phone battery finally gave out. My only option now, praying for help. I closed my eyes for a moment to allow them to adjust to the change in light and almost didn't get them open again. However, as I managed to pull them open I could see a soft warm glow coming from the cottage window. "Thank you, Jesus," I muttered through chattering teeth. I didn't close my eyes for fear the image before me would vanish into the inky darkness and forced myself to plunge forward. 'I am Declan Douglas, I will not die in my own driveway during a blizzard.' I proclaimed loudly in my head.

By the time I made it to the front door of the cottage, I could hardly move. My strength was fading fast now that safety was within reach. Mustering my remaining energy, I began to kick at the door. No light came from within, leaving me to wonder what light guided me safely to her door. At this moment I don't care and didn't question it further, I had made it. The thought then occurs to me, what if Hamish had Gabriella stay at the main house? I kicked harder, then rested a moment to gather more strength. If it came down to it, I would break in. I wasn't going to get this far only to die in the cold. I prepared mentally to force my way in when the porch light came on. I lifted my head up. Soon after the door flies open and I fall in, right into the arms of Gabriella. I don't care. I made it. The warm air inside her cottage envelopes me like a welcoming friend.

Chapter Seventeen

Declan

She is talking to me, but I can't understand a word coming out of her mouth. 'Thank you, dear lord, for helping me to safety.' I send up to the powers of heaven with every fiber of my being. My brain registers what Gabriella is saying, sit, she wants me to sit down. I comply, sitting on the bench by the front door. I vaguely feel her jerking at the laces of my boots. When she manages to free my other foot, I hear the soft soothing tones of her voice, but only catch clipped words, ' stay here,' I couldn't go anywhere, except maybe to lay down where I sat. I think I am nodding in response to her demand, but truly don't know. I tried to talk, but nothing came out.

When she returned moments later from where ever she ran off to, she began taking my clothes off. In any other situation, this would've been awkward, however, now, I wanted nothing more than to be rid of these cold, damp fabrics that sucked the life force from me. Gabriella freed me of the sweater and button down, before wrapping a towel around my shoulders and another over my head. It felt like heaven. Tugging on my forearms with a demanding tone in her voice, I realize she wants me to stand. I manage to get up and hear her say 'bedroom.' I look at her in confusion and focus on her mouth as she explains, "I need to get these wet pants off you and get you warm." I don't understand why she needs me in the bedroom for that, but at this moment a bed, even her bed, sounded rather good. I could not say what all took place next, but the next thing I knew I lay flat on my back with Gabriella tucking a warmed blanket around me. If I thought I could get away with it, I would've grabbed her and kissed her. She more than likely would slug me, but it would be worth it in this moment.

Chapter Eighteen

Gabriella

I woke to a thump...thump pause thump...thump pause on what sounded like the front door. Who in their right mind would be out in a storm like this? I glance at the thermostat on my way through the living room. It read seventy. I make a mental note to put another log on the fire before going back to bed. I peer out the front window and see the dark figure of a big man standing on the porch. I reach over to flip the light on as he started to kick the door again. He paused in his movement as the area surrounding him illuminated and lifted his head just enough for me to see his strained face.

I jerked the door open and he stumbled through grabbing on to me for support. "Oh my god, Declan! I got you!" I get him all the way inside and shut the door behind him. A quick head to toe glance and it is quite clear this is a life and death situation. My focus changed, and I went into 'triage nurse' mode. "Declan, I need you to sit down on the bench." I know it is bad when he complies without an argument. I fall to my knees in front of him and start the process of pulling off the boots and socks that are frozen near solid to his feet. "Declan stay with me." I plead. He gives a slight nod of his head letting me know he is with me. "Declan, I am going to go get some towels I will be right back." While in the bath I moved with adrenaline-laced speed, grabbing an extra blanket and tossing it in the dryer.

When I return, I notice he is trying to stay upright, as tremors wreak havoc on his muscles, but it's difficult for him. "Come on Declan, I need you to help me get these clothes off." I start with his gloves, coat, scarf before pulling off his sweater and shirt. I hear him let out a contented sigh as I wrapped a towel around his shoulders and drape another over his head. The next part would be tricky. "Declan you need to get up." I not only see but can feel it takes everything he has to get up. A moment later I decided this is going to be much simpler to do once. "Declan, I want you to hold on to me. We are moving into the bedroom." Our eyes meet and though he is weak and fighting to stay conscious, I can see confusion cross his face. I explain, "I have to get these wet pants off you and get you warm. Look, I know it is hard for you, but I need you to trust me a little right now." He nods his acceptance and begins moving with me. As if we are at a sixth-grade dance, he is leaning down on my shoulders and I am shuffling us backward a step at a time.

It is a slow process getting him across the room and to the bedroom. Once he is standing at the side of the bed I ask, "Can you stand here for a few seconds on your own?" he nods, and I dart back into the bath to retrieve the warmed blanket. I lay it on the bed within reach then I straighten in front of him. Without any preamble, I unbuckle his belt, undo the button, unzip the fly and slide his trousers down his hips. It was a surprise to find the man commando underneath his pants, but I am grateful. That is one less piece of clothing to deal with in this nightmare. Once his pants are around his ankles, I set him on the edge of the bed, drop to my knees and pull the frozen damp mess from him in one swift movement. I manage to get him into the bed and flat on his back. I tuck the warmed blanket around him and inquired, "What in God's name were you doing out there?"

With great difficulty, he managed to speak one word, "Accident."

The blood drains from my face, but I continue, "You were in an accident?" He nods. "Did you hit your head?" He shakes his head no. I open the nightstand drawer and retrieve my mini mag light. "Declan, I am going to shine a light in your eyes to double check, okay?" He nods his head yes. Both pupils reacted as they should. I moved to do a visual and sensory exam of his torso and arms. His skin is pink from the cold, but not concerning. I look to his hands which are an angry red color, checking the capillary return of each finger. I pull the blanket back up and move to his lower extremities. "Declan, I am going to check your legs."

"Okay." He rasps out. That was a good sign, at least he tried to communicate verbally. I go through the same sweep of my hands checking the cap return. His feet were purple in color rather than red like his hands, which concerned me. I needed to get him warmed up. "Declan, I am going to layer blankets over you." Once we get the shivering under control I want to put you in a warm bath."

"Okay", he rasps out again. I move up to look at his face. His lips are dry and cracked. "Declan, I need you to stay awake and talking to me. Can you do that?"

"Yes." His one-word answers are better than none.

"How long were you out there? What time did you wreck the Rover?" I inquire.

"Don't know." He thinks for a few seconds before answering, "six thirty-seven."

I look at the clock it read eleven thirteen. This process of getting him to the bed took thirty to forty minutes, which means for four and a half to five hours he was exposed to the brutal elements. "I'll be right back." I ran back to the stove, tossing three logs in and turn up the forced air blower. Sprinting into the kitchen, I retrieve a large glass of water and a straw. "You still with me?" I called to the man bundled in blankets on my bed.

"Yes, thank you, Gab." Only one other time has he referred to me as Gab, it felt odd...touching. He called me something that no one else did. I shook that thought away, I needed to focus on getting him stable.

I watch with elation as the light of life starts to flicker in his eyes and feel a bit of hope that my efforts are helping. I open my nightstand drawer again and pull out a tube of lip balm. Using my finger, I dab a small amount on my finger and begin to rub it into his lips. He jerks back slightly, and I realize I didn't tell him first. "Sorry, it is lip balm. Your lips are dry and cracking. They will be painful if I don't get them moisturized." He nods. "Do you think you can help me to set you up in the bed? You need to drink some water to keep you hydrated or things may start to go south." He pushes up slightly and I move into a hug-style position helping him to set up straight. He groans a bit. "I am sorry Declan, I know you hurt, and you are cold. If we didn't need to get fluids in you I would let it go."

"It's okay" he rasps in my ear. Once he is steady, I grab all the pillows and stack them behind him. I ease him back and pull the blankets back around him. I notice his shivering slowed somewhat, but his eyes are still glazed looking.

I grab the water and place the straw at his lips, "We will start off slow just take a few sips and then we will take a break." He nods his understanding. I study his face carefully as he takes the first sip making sure he doesn't choke. I let him take a couple more sips before placing the glass back on the table. "It feels like the stove is heating up, I am going to go slow it down a bit." I move back into the living room and to the wood stove. I turn the intake to low and shut the damper down. A quick glance at the thermostat tells me it is seventy-five in the front room now. As I move back to the bedroom I say a prayer, "Please let him pull through. The man is arrogant and pompous, but he does not deserve this." I go through the bedroom to the bathroom and turn the small electric heater in there on high. I could hear the wind picking up and the freezing rain pelting the metal roof in a growing steady crescendo of taps. I am thankful he made it when he did. Listening to the weather outside, if he'd delayed his trip an hour, this situation would be much different.

I would not be surprised if we lost power before the sunrises. Considering this, I move back into the bedroom. Declan is following my movements with his eyes. "The storm is picking up force. Do you want to attempt a bath or chance it until tomorrow?

He considers my question before answering, "Now." I give a single nod of my head and go back to the bathroom. I toss two towels and another blanket into the dryer to warm before beginning to fill the tub with water. I lay out a bar of soap, washcloth, and my shampoo and conditioner where I can reach them easily from the tub side.

I shut the water off and move back to the bedroom, "Are you ready for this?"

"No," he answers but there is a smile in his eyes now. I pull the blankets back, help him swing his legs over the side of the bed and assume the hug position as I help him to stand, wrapping the not so warm now blanket around him. In the back of my mind, I am fighting the thoughts that are screaming at me he is naked. I went into nurse mode and will not let such trivial notions get in the way of caring for this man.

Not letting go, I move backward toward the bathroom door giving him words of praise and encouragement as we shuffle across the room. Helping steady him, not even thinking, I step into the warm water and before he follows, I warn, "It may be painful at first, as the blood starts to rush back to your toes." He nods and places his foot in the water, hissing through clenched teeth. I tighten my grip on him as he brings the other foot in and hisses again. "You understand it's going to feel that way when you sit down too."

He answers with less rasp and more of a pained groan, "yes." I ease him down into the water and once he is situated I step out. It is at this point I realize I am in nothing but a tee shirt and boxer shorts, but I must admit I am glad, otherwise I would be a soaking wet mess. I move toward the door as he rasps out with an edge of panic in his voice, "Wait. Don't leave me."

I look back at him, "I won't be far, I am going to remove the damp linens from the bed and put dry ones on. I will be right back to help you wash." He nods weakly. That short trek took a lot out of him, it was plain in his physical appearance. Knowing he wouldn't be able to sit there long, I make quick work of the bedding and decided to grab all his wet clothing before I return to him.

Upon re-entering the bathroom with my load of wash, Declan's closed eyes fly open. "Are you okay?" I ask him.

"Yes, now that the tingling stopped." His voice is still quite gruff sounding.

"Good." I kneel next to the tub, grab the washcloth and the bar of soap, dip it in the water and lather up the cloth. I set the bar to the side and begin washing his neck, down his chest and move on to his arms.

"How..." he starts to ask but the rest of his words catch in his throat.

I keep up the scrubbing, but finish his question, "how did I know what to do?"

"Yes."

"Well Mr. Douglas," I smirk, "when I got out of high school I joined the Army and became a nurse." I grabbed a large cup I used for rinsing and asked him to set up, so I could wash his hair. Steadying him with one arm, I pour three cups of water over his upturned head. As I started to massage the shampoo into his hair he moaned. I froze, "Does this hurt you?"

"No. It feels...good, nobody has ever washed my hair before."

I scoff, "What about the barber, when he cuts your hair?"

"No, the barber uses a spray to wet it."

I rinse his hair, then start with the conditioner. "Sorry if it smells to girlie for you, but it is all I have."

He moans again, "What is that?"

"What?"

"What did you just put in my hair?"

"Oh, it's conditioner. You don't condition your hair?" I cannot believe a man with his gorgeous dark locks does not know what conditioner is.

"No"

"Well, it will make it soft, manageable and less tangled when combing it out later." I sound all perky in my reply just like a commercial.

"Really?" he sounded like the concept was as foreign to him as haggis was to me.

"Yes really. Are you joking? Have you never heard of conditioner? It's right next to the shampoo in most stores." I see the frown that is ever present on his face appear.

"Molly places an order weekly for my grocery and household needs. I don't actually go myself, there usually isn't time. If I need anything special, I tell Molly." He almost sounds embarrassed that he doesn't do his own shopping.

To change the subject to something a little more pertinent to the situation we are in, rather than his personal care, I asked, "Speaking of Molly, were they expecting you back this evening? Do I need to call them?"

"No. The last they knew I would fly in Monday. To my knowledge, Tim is the only person who knows I came home, and he won't be concerned until Monday afternoon if he doesn't hear from me. I thought I could make it home and I would've if something hadn't

jumped out in front of me, that is how I ended up wrecking the Rover."

"I will wait to call Hamish in the morning and let him know the situation. That way if people start looking for you he will know where you are." Declan gave a single nod before I gave his head a final rinse. The power began to flicker. "Let's get you rinsed and back to bed." I reach in skimming his thigh as I pulled the plug to let the water drain. I remember something my mother used to do when the power might go out and shoved it right back in.

"What are you doing?" He shifts his eyes to the hole and then to me, puzzled.

"If the power goes out the well won't work. I can use this water to flush the toilet." He stares at me as if I sprouted horns from my head. "Trust me, I know." He shakes his head as I move to the dryer to retrieve the warmed towels. I step back into the tub with him repeating the process in reverse that we took getting him in. I do a quick pat down then grab the blanket I warmed and wrapped it around him.

"I am much warmer now." He says barely audible, looking down into my eyes, just like in that stupid dream.

"Good," I whisper back, then look away to start the slow dance back to the bed.

Getting back to the bed went much faster than going in. He slowly sat down on the side of the bed. "Before you lay down let's get some more water in you. Do you want some crackers or toast? I don't want to give you too much, just in case."

"Just in case of what?" concern coating his voice.

"Just in case it decides it wants to come back up. I can handle a lot of bodily fluid, but vomit is not one of them."

He half smiled, but seconds later his features turned serious, "Speaking of bodily fluids." I quirk a questioning eyebrow at him, "You're going to kill me, but I should have used the facilities while we were in there."

I give him an exaggerated roll of my eyes, "I will let it slide this time, but next time there will be consequences." This time his eyebrow quirks. Before he can question I say, "Hold on a second. I move to the dresser and grab the biggest, most stretchy pair of shorts I own. "I know these are going to be a little snug, but I can't have you flopping around in my bed all night." I looked up in shock, not believing I just said it like that. My neck and face begin to heat as the reddening blush creeps up, "that is not exactly what I meant...what I mean is..."

He is smirking at me completely enjoying my slip. "If it won't be too much trouble, I would prefer to be flopping around and not confined while I sleep."

I know I just turned as red as his winter cold hands. For Pete's sake! "Fine, let's get you to the bathroom." At least I will be sleeping on the couch. A shuffling we go.

Once back to the bed I get him covered up and glance at the clock, twelve forty-eight. "I think you should be okay to sleep. I will be on the couch if you need anything."

He grabs my wrist, in the same instant the power goes out. "I would feel better if you stayed close." I reach to the bedside table using the backlight of my phone to find the lighter to light the candle sitting there.

"You want me to sleep in the bed...with you?" He has lost his mind if he thinks I am getting in this bed with him.

"We are adults and I don't think in my condition you have anything to worry about. Not to mention you don't even like me."

I consider this for a moment, uncomfortable with the idea of being in bed with Declan Douglas, but on the other hand, should something happen in the night, it would be better to be close. "Alright, let me go put another log in the stove and make sure the door is locked."

Ten minutes later I am sliding into bed with a man for the first time in over a year and it must be a man I can't stand. Well, that isn't all true, but I push those thoughts out of my mind. I am Nurse Gabriella right now. "Are you comfortable?" I asked him.

"Quite. Thank you."

"You're welcome." I prayed this wouldn't be the start of awkward pillow talk. Surely, he'd be too exhausted. In all the time I spent in this man's company, I could never imagine being in this kind of situation with him. Talking before bed couldn't be more wrong, on so many levels.

"Good night Gabriella."

"Good night Declan." I sighed in silent relief, knowing there will be no more conversation. I stayed awake until I could hear his breathing move into a slow steady pace, telling me he fell asleep. Seconds later I followed.

Chapter Nineteen

Gabriella

I woke up feeling warm and snuggled in closer, taking in a deep breath and exhaling. I slept really well, better than I have in months. I move my hand up the firm warm surface on the side of the bed. My eyes fly open, but I am frozen in place. In my sleep, I managed to snuggle up to Declan's warm body. Snuggle might be an understatement. He is still laying on his back with his arm wrapped firmly around my shoulders. My head is on his chest and my leg thrown over him, with my knee...oh my, is that...No, that can't be his... Needing to get out of this position and not wanting to wake him, I start to gently pull back when his arm tightens around me.

"Don't move," His morning gravelly voice says, and I tense every muscle. "you're so warm." He explains.

"Are you still cold?" Concern laced my voice.

"Not like I was. My feet are still a tad icy." He slides his foot up against mine.

"Oh my God, they are cold!" I squeak, and he chuckles in earnest amusement. This is the first time this sound has come from him in my presence. I take a moment to soak in how nice it is to hear. During the few hours of sleep I sprawled myself across this detestable man, who isn't fond of me, and he is playing footsie with me. How in the world did we even get into this position? I look up at him as just enough light is shining through the window that I can make out his shadowed face. He looks down at me and says in quiet seriousness, "You were amazing last night." He is talking about taking care of him, he is talking about taking care of him, I repeat in my head before swallowing hard with the discomfort I felt.

"I am glad I was here to help you. Would you like some coffee?" He shakes his head no, his eyes holding mine captive, "Tea?" Again, with the shaking of the head. "Breakfast?" This time he leans down and with the softness of a rose petal, brushes his lips across mine. Butterflies take off in my stomach. What in the...I reach my hand up to stroke his cheek. As soon as my hand touches his face I find he is burning up. "Declan, you're running a fever."

"I am?" He says in a darkly seductive voice.

I push away from him, "Yes. I need to get some more water in you and some Tylenol or ibuprofen." His fever concerned me, but my voice stuttered with the uncomfortableness of this situation instead of the firmness I wanted to convey. I needed to get out of this bed before he decided to kiss me again.

"Are you saying I am hot?" He winked at me.

"I am saying I think you are delirious with a fever." I should've known. When he held me closer to his body, rather than push me away, it should've registered it was out of character for him. "Let me up." I try to push away again. He squeezes me for a second longer and I don't think he is going to let me go. He places a delicate kiss on my forehead and releases his grip. Declan Douglas is kissing me. This would be one for the books and I bet he will never admit such behavior from himself.

I moved into the bathroom to rinse and refill his water glass, but as soon as my hand hits the faucet, I remember the power is out. I head for the kitchen to retrieve water from the pitcher in the fridge and put a liter bottle in that I bought at the store. I return to the bath and pull out a bottle of Ibuprofen from the medicine cabinet and drop two in my hand. Grabbing my thermometer from the drawer, I take in a deep breath. His kisses shouldn't muddle my brain as they did, but it felt nice. I took in another deep breath to calm my racing heart. With all the items in hand, I went back into the bedroom. A quick glance at the bed and I know something is very wrong. In the few minutes it took me to gather the things in my hands, Declan is buried under the covers, shivering again and a slight sheen of sweat beaded on his forehead. I speed up my steps set everything down. He looks up at me his eyes are starting to glaze again. "I am cold." He chatters out.

"I am going to take your temperature." His eyes close, "Declan, look at me." He opens them slightly. I run the device over his temporal area. 102.4 degrees Fahrenheit. "Declan, I am going to need you to take some medicine." He nods and pushes himself to a sitting position taking the pills and then washing them down with water. "Go back to sleep," I say to him. He scoots back down in the bed and closes his eyes. I pull the covers back up over him. My cell phone is laying on the nightstand where I plugged it in to charge last night. Thank goodness it fully charged before the power went out. I noted the time, 5:45 in the morning. I would give him more Ibuprofen in six to eight hours.

As fast as I could move, I went into the living room, adding a few more logs to the simmering coals. Glancing at the thermostat, which read sixty-nine, I flipped the blower dial to off, giving the stove time to heat up. Without the heater running in the bathroom, I would need to get the temperature up to keep Declan warm or move him to the couch. Given his tall frame that wouldn't be comfortable in the least. Once I ensure the fire took off, I went into the kitchen to heat a kettle of water for the instant coffee I picked up at the grocery store. It was not my favorite, but no power meant no electric coffee pot, so I took the next best thing. Considering the man in my bed, I filled a large pot with water to wash up with and placed it on a burner to warm. With all my tasks handled for the moment, I sat down at the kitchenette and watched the snow fall. I pull up the Weather Channel app on my phone and see light snow will come down all day. Seeing the beautiful scene out my window, I stood and took a picture. I sent it to my Mom and Diana, with the tag of beautiful winter weather in Scotland. I sat back down with my coffee and think about my current predicament, a sick Declan in my bed. I chuckle to myself and shoot off another text, just to my sister this time, 'lucky for me there is a man in my bed keeping me warm' and added a winky face emoji, that ought to wake her up. I then go into settings, put it to low battery mode, and reduce the backlight power to conserve as much of the battery as I can.

At seven o'clock, I call Hamish to tell him what happened last night and Declan's condition this morning. "Oh, lass. There's another storm coming in. The way they are talking it's gonna be three or four days before it will move out enough to clear the roads. Do you think you can manage him?" Hamish's voice gave away his amusement at my current predicament.

I laugh knowing Hamish is aware of the tension that runs between Declan and myself. "I am not concerned about being stuck here with him in the slightest. My concern is for his fever. I picked up enough supplies in town the other day to keep us covered for a couple of weeks, so it's not a worry either. The propane tank and the woodshed are both full. I just wanted you to be aware of the situation and not calling for help."

Hamish laughed. "I will call Tim, his assistant to have his calls picked up by the answering service. Not too much happens during the winter. He is usually up brooding in his office most of the winter going over reports and the like."

"Oh well," I reply, "he can lay here and brood just fine."

"Gab?" I hear Declan weakly, but urgently holler from the bedroom.

"Okay Hamish, I need to run, he is calling. I will call if there is any change."

I hang up with Hamish and stroll into the bedroom to see Declan sitting on the side of the bed, shoulders slumped forward and a green pallor to his skin. I dart into the bathroom and retrieve the trash can. Just in time, as I place it in front of him, liquid shoots out of his mouth. He groans miserably. "I am so..." gag, "sorry..." dry heave, "Gab."

Rubbing circles on his back I speak soothingly. "You have nothing to be sorry for. You're sick and lucky that is all you are" He straightens his shoulders a little. "Better?" He nods. "Stay sitting a minute." I walk through the bathroom and into the kitchen to grab the water pitcher from the frig, going back the way I had come, I grabbed a washrag off the shelf, before returning to Declan. I fill his glass, pouring a little of the cool water on the cloth to wipe his forehead and mouth. "Do you think you can drink some water?" He nods his head as his weakened muscles begin to quiver. He manages to drink half the glass before I pull it away. "Is that setting okay on your stomach?"

"Yeah. I feel horrible." His chin falls toward his chest.

"Do you want to try to eat some crackers? We really need to keep something in your stomach." He agrees, and I head for the kitchen once more, thankful this isn't an overly large house. When I return, Declan looks as if he is about to fall to the floor. Kneeling in front of him I hand him a saltine. As he nibbles on it, I begin to tell him about my conversation with Hamish and about the second storm that is moving in. By the time I finish telling him the information he ate three crackers and drank his water. He helps me to situate him back in the bed and I note his color is a little better, but not by much.

"I am going to go out and bring more wood into the house and collect some snow." He looks at me puzzled so I explain, "I will melt the snow for water to flush the toilet. With no power for the well, we are going to run out sooner than I expected. Not flushing the toilet is not an option. He nods in understanding. He stares at the bathroom wall behind me and I see the worry lines start to crease his forehead. Without thinking I run my thumb over it, "what is troubling you?"

He lays still for a moment more before he explains, "I have to go to the bathroom." I didn't understand why that would concern him.

"Why does that make you look worried? We have done it before."

"I may need to be in there longer this time."

I look at him understanding what he is getting at and tilt my head to the side, "Seriously? Are you going to get shy on me now? I've stripped you, bathed you, and held a bucket while you retched, I think we are beyond being embarrassed over bodily functions." He blushed. It seemed I had finally knocked a bit of Declan Douglas's smugness out of him.

He shakes his head in disbelief. "You are a different kind of woman Gabriella Fairmont."

"As long as different is in a uniquely satisfying way, I'll take it. Now, come on. I'll leave you to your peace with your bucket and go do my chores. I'll check back in with you every few minutes to make sure you're okay and not laying on the floor in a puddle of your own drool." He smirks up at me, nods, and we begin the process of walking across the room. Once in the bathroom I leave him to his peace.

It must be hard for an alpha male who controls every aspect of his life to find himself in a position of complete and utter helplessness. In some ways, I feel sorry for this man who can barely hold himself up at the bathroom sink, but on the other hand, it serves him right. I thought back to our first meeting. He was an arrogant self-righteous jerk to me. Not even caring what I had to say. Now, he is at my mercy. Not that I enjoy his torture, but karma, what goes around comes around.

I make two trips to the woodshed and back before I check on him. "I am okay, but I am not done." I make two more passes to the woodshed, then start filling my buckets with the snow to dump in the tub. Bringing the second round of buckets in, I hear a loud thump and run to the bathroom, flinging open the door in a full-on panic, "Declan are you oka..."

Declan is still sitting there looking at me mortified, "For god sake woman what in the ever-loving hell are you doing?"

"I heard...sorry...I thought...I thought you fell." I make my way back out of the bathroom and into the bedroom.

I hear him call, "I am about done. Give me a few minutes." I didn't utter another word. I decided to tidy up the bed while he was otherwise, occupied. In my intrusion moments ago, I noticed that he didn't look well at all and figured he more than likely would want to slip back into bed when he finished. With that thought, I heard the toilet flush. I waited for him to call for me and continued with straightening the bedding. Several minutes passed and I still didn't hear a sound. I chewed on my lower lip debating what to do. This situation was the most awkward situation ever and I didn't want to burst through the door on him again.

My fist raised to the door, about to tap, when I heard him call, "Gab?" Standing just outside the door, I barely heard his beckon.

I moved closer to the door before calling out, "I am here Declan."

A couple of seconds passed before he hesitantly called out, "Could I have a wet washcloth to clean my face?"

Of course, he could, but did he want me to tell him where they were, or should I go in. Then I remembered that the power was out. "I am coming in. Are you ready?" I could hear him shifting a bit before he gave me the all clear to enter. The expression on his face told me he felt miserable and weak. Taking everything in I noticed he tried to pull a towel over himself, but it appeared he lost the gumption halfway through the process. Without a word, I grabbed several cloths from the cabinet and went to the kitchen stove where the pot of warm water sat. I dipped the cloth into the water, rang them out, and went back to the bathroom.

Upon touching the warm wet material, he looked to me with confusion, "I thought the power was out?"

"It is. I warmed water in a pot on the stove." At that moment I realize what the thumping noise I had heard earlier was when I rushed in on him. Declan flushed the toilet and refilled it with the leftover bath water. The noise I heard was him replacing the tank lid. He tried to wipe his face but seemed to be having difficulty keeping his arm up. Without preamble I stepped closer, took the rag from him and began to wash his face and down his neck, the terry cloth catching on his beard stubble. He closed his eyes and swayed a bit. "Declan, what else do you want washed?"

"That's good." He said as he opened his eyes and his emerald green eyes pierced me, straight through my heart. Without taking my eyes from his, I reached down and grabbed the towel he pulled over himself, "I have the bed ready for you." I spoke in a hushed tone as I held out my hand to help him up. As he stood I slid the towel around his waist. He placed his trembling hands on my shoulders and our eyes still locked on each other, I asked, "Are you still cold?"

He shook his head, "No, just weak. I am beginning to think I may have picked up the flu on the flight in. It was just aggravated by my little walk in the weather."

"It is possible, I suppose." We began moving back to the bed and forced my eyes away from his mesmerizing stare to glance over my shoulder. Once he was back in the bed again, I asked, "Would you like some broth or crackers? Maybe some toast?"

Declan considers this a moment before answering, "Maybe after a bit. If I could have a drink of water that would be enough for now."

I got him settled and went to refresh his glass of water. He drank it, then lay back in the bed. I placed my hand on his forehead and felt he was still quite warm, but I couldn't give him any more medication at the moment. As I pulled the cover-up over him I spoke as a mother would to a child, "Get some rest and call if you need anything." He mumbled an unintelligible response and soon began to snore. I sat there a moment longer than I should have, watching him. He is without a doubt a handsome man, even sick. The woman who ended up with Declan Douglas would be a lucky woman indeed, if she wasn't American. With that final thought, I exited the bedroom, closing the door behind me with a silent click.

Chapter Twenty

Declan

I awoke to the sweet aromas of breakfast cooking. I had been in and out of consciousness for at least two days, or so I believed. Gabriella took exceptional care of me during this ordeal. Of course, I lacked actual first-hand knowledge of medical staff, however, if I ever needed to be in a medical facility for any period of time, I hoped my caregiver was at least half as good as my Gab. 'My Gab', I scoffed to myself. Where did that thought come from? In however long I had been here, in all honesty, I could say my opinion of the woman had definitely changed significantly, but to say she was mine, well nothing could be further from the truth.

I lay there a few minutes listening in silence to see exactly where she might be in the house but heard nothing. I wanted to call out to her, but the past few days, she fussed over me enough. Never in all my life, even as a child, had I never needed someone to care for me as Gab had done. I certainly never needed to have help going to and from the bathroom. With that thought, I decided, today would be the day, I didn't need to lean on her to get to the blasted bathroom. Swinging my legs over the side of the bed, I sat there a moment to gather my strength and waited for the room to stop spinning.

I reconsidered calling for her to bring me a bowl of warm water to wash up with when I got a look of myself in the mirror. "Dear Lord in heaven," I said to my reflection as I ran the palm of my hand over what appeared to be five days' worth of beard growth. Thinking back over my trip to America that would be about right. I didn't shave the morning I left in order to catch an earlier flight to Edinburgh. At that point, a full day passed since I last shaved and given my current predicament it would be a few more days before I would get the chance. Grabbing a towel from the linen closet to wrap around me, I headed for the kitchen and what smelt like bangers and drop scones.

As I made it to the door frame of the kitchen I froze in place and my heart skipped a beat. Gabriella stood at the stove in an oversized tee shirt that hit about her knees, bare feet, and her short hair covered with one of those blue paisley rags on her head. The sunlight shining through the window cast an almost ethereal glow around her. She looked...like an angel. I shook my head to clear these thoughts from my head and cleared my throat to announce my presence. She whirled around splattering scone batter across the stove, counter, and floors, a scream catching in her throat. Her panic filled eyes take a split second before recognition dawns. She spoke with a slight gasp, "Good lord Declan, you scared me!" She turned back to the stove and began wiping up the mess.

Still caught up in her beauty I took her in for a few seconds more before speaking, "I think I would like to set up for a bit. I think I've been abed long enough." She didn't say a word just nodded in understanding while removing the breakfast items from the skillet.

"You okay?" She questioned as she moves toward me. I held a hand up and moved further into the kitchen. I reached for a chair at the table and right before I sat, she spoke.

"Before you sit, can I get you something to put on?" I glance down at myself and then back to her. She couldn't possibly own clothing that I would be able to wear. I stood thoughtfully quiet, considering this predicament when she explained, "I have an oversized tee shirt and a pair of cut off sweats that may fit you." She stood thoughtfully for a moment before smirking, "I highly doubt you flop around the main house all day. I can't imagine Hamish or Molly would care too much for that."

I just shook my head and smiled as she walked past me toward the bedroom. I followed more slowly, then sat on the side of the bed. She turned to face me with a shirt and a pair of shorts in hand, "The clothing you showed up in is still in a pile on the washing machine, but I am pretty sure they are going to be a lost cause."

"More than likely." I agreed as I reached my hand out for the clothes she held in hers. "Well, we can just consider ourselves even now."

She scrunches up her nose, "How do you figure that?"

Chuckling at her indignant response, I explained, "Not too long ago you were sitting in my kitchen wearing my clothes."

She stared at me, debating her next words, then dryly responded, "Well, if we are keeping score, you owe me. I have taken care of you for the past several days."

I don't know what came over me, but something about Gabriella Fairmont made the kid in me want to come out and play, so I asked, "You want me to give you a bath?"

Her face became a pretty shade of pink, "No I do not want you to give me a bath!" She tossed the clothing items at me, "Put the clothes on and I will serve you up some pancakes and sausage." She walked out the door shaking her head and mumbling, "Give me a bath."

Chapter Twenty-One

Declan

I watched over my shoulder as Gabriella exits the bedroom to the safety of the kitchen. Once she is out of sight I take a second to steady myself before trying to dress. If I didn't know any better I would've thought a truck ran me over. I didn't feel like cracking jokes, honestly, I never poked fun at anyone, but Gabriella did something to me. She made me angry and playful at the same time. I wanted to tell her to leave but hold her in the same breath. She could blame it on the fever, but a few days ago, when I woke up to her warm body laying half on top of me, I didn't want to move, I didn't want her to move! I shouldn't have kissed her, but at that moment it felt right, more so than I ever felt with anyone else.

The past few days were a blur, but I knew she slept in the bed next to me watching over me. I must admit, at least to myself, with her being near I slept better than I had in years. Of course, I couldn't speak for her, but she looked more rested this morning than when I first laid eyes on her. I thought for a moment about going back to the main house and my own big bed; just the thought made me a little...empty. Gabriella was an attractive woman, no doubt about that, but what I felt was more than a physical attraction. It was simply, her. The more time I spent with her, the closer I wanted to be to her, which was utterly ridiculous. She was right, that fever must be doing a number on my brain.

I look at the tee shirt and pulled it on. It was a little snug, but not terribly so. Clearly, it was a man's shirt by the style. With that, another thought crossed my mind, I hoped this wasn't her husband's, though she too wore an oversized tee shirt this morning. Regardless, I would take care not to spill anything on it. I couldn't imagine she would give me something that precious to her, but I sure wasn't going to ask. I would just play it safe. The shorts, on the other hand, undoubtedly hers. For the first time in my life, I wished I wore boxers. These were snug to the point they were a tad uncomfortable, but as she said I couldn't be flopping all over the house. I chuckle to myself recalling the night she saved me, she had been so embarrassed at her own words. This morning though, she fired them right off like we were old friends.

I sat on the bed a few more minutes trying to gather the strength to get up. I wasn't entirely sure I could eat just yet, but I needed to get up and move around. I took in a deep breath and stood. The room spun for a second and then I slowly made my way back to the kitchen.

Upon my re-entry, Gabriella turned from the stove to look at me. I could see the amusement playing in her eyes at my state of dress, but she never said a word. I sat down in a chair at the kitchenette and she placed a steaming mug of coffee down in front of me. "Thank you. I hope it stays down."

Grimacing she responded, "Yes. If it feels like it may upset your stomach I can make you a cup of peppermint tea. That is what my mom always gave my sister and me when we were sick."

Hoping I looked sincere I told her. "Thanks for everything you have done for me. I hate to think what would have happened if you weren't here."

She smiled at me. "Is that your way of apologizing for being an arrogant ass?"

I couldn't help but smile back. I shrugged, "If you'd like to think that you go right ahead." I took a few small sips of the coffee and it felt like it would stay down, but I gave it a minute all the same. Placing my mug down I asked, "You by chance didn't charge my phone before the power went out, did you?

She looks puzzled for a second. "I didn't find a cell on you Declan. Did you have it with you?"

I played through the events of that night in my head and nodded. "I am sure I did. It was about dead, but I used the flashlight app to see where I was going. When it died, I could see a glow from your window, but I don't remember what I did with it. I really need to check in with my assistant."

She looked confused, "You saw a glow from the window? Declan, I had been in bed for hours before you showed up. There wouldn't have been any lights on." She pondered that a moment before continuing, "I talked to Hamish earlier. He is going to call your assistant and have all the calls go to your answering system." She turned back to me with a plate of three scones, a banger, silverware, and syrup. She sat them down in front of me. "I will understand if you can't eat them, but you should at least try."

"Thank you." I realize I have said 'thank you' more to this woman in the past few days than anyone else in my life. "So, it sounds like Hamish has that under control."

She nods as she heads back to the stove. "I wasn't sure what kind of shape you would be in, so I hope you don't think I overstepped my bounds. I thought it was for the best. You really did need to rest after what you've been through. I am not too sure you still don't need a few more days. "

No, I didn't think she overstepped at all. If I were being honest it was a considerate thing to do. "Did you say there was another storm coming?"

"I did. Hamish said we could be stuck here for three or four days given the prediction."

I felt horrible and sore all over, but I didn't tell her that. Instead, I offered, "Is there anything I can do to help you?"

Chapter Twenty-Two

Gabriella

I almost laughed aloud at his question, but I managed to keep myself under control. The man looked half dead on his feet. He also appeared like he could vomit at any moment. "No, but thanks anyway. I grew up surviving winter ice storms. If you don't want to go back to bed, you could go sit on the couch." I considered a few seconds trying to think of what he could do. "I have a crossword and a word find book. Other than that, I am pretty sparse on entertainment."

He looks around the kitchen and into the living room. He floored me when he said, "We could sit and talk, get to know each other a little better."

I have been here months now, almost killed because of him and now he wants to get to know me. "O-kay? What do you want to know?"

He looked thoughtful for a moment. "Why did you come to Scotland? How did you end up in Dochas?"

I laughed half-heartedly. "Wow. You want to get right to the hard stuff."

He frowned, crinkling the skin between his brows. "I'm sorry. I thought that would be an easy question." He sounded completely confused by my statement.

I motioned for him to move to the living room. He sat on the couch and I moved to the wood stove to add another log to the fire. Letting out a heavy sigh, I answered him. "I chose to come to Scotland because I fell in love with the images and the history of the country while doing a research project in school. I swore that someday I would come here." I paused and thoughtfully looked out the window. In a hushed tone I added, "I needed to get away from...home. I needed to just...get away. The first place I thought of was here." I looked back to him. "However, Edinburgh wasn't what I expected. I spent a few days there and then searched for a smaller community that I could get the real feel of Scotland from. A couple of days later I travelled to Dochas." I sat in a chair across from him. "How about you? Why are you here?"

He laughed. "This is where I grew up. My parents divorced when I was seven and I lived in New York for a while with my mum. When I hit my teen years I moved back with my Dad. This is his family estate and passed down to me by tradition. It has always passed to the first-born son. Regrettably, that tradition may end with me unless I give it up to my younger brother."

Without even thinking I asked, "Why aren't you married?" I slapped my hand over my mouth. "Sorry, that was rude."

He shook his head. "No, not at all. I haven't found a woman worth settling down with. Most of them are either settled wherever they are at and don't want to move, or they aren't right in the head, like Samantha. I need a woman who would be content living in the middle of nowhere and not mind taking frequent business trips with me. A woman who is headstrong, but willing to stay home and raise children if we should be blessed with any." He finished and looked at me directly, "Tell me about your husband."

I looked at him unspeaking for a long moment. "Daniel. His name was Daniel. We met in Kindergarten, fell in love in middle school and were together ever since. We joined the military together. When we came home he went to work and I stayed home and raised our two boys." I felt a tear fall from my eye but kept going. "He was the love of my life. They all were. Everything I did was for my boys. Daniel and I were a completed pair. He knew what I was thinking, and I could finish his sentences. Oh, we argued some, but it was over little stuff. I couldn't even tell you what it was now, it wasn't important." Tears were streaming down my face now as I looked out the window. "My last memory, the last words he ever said to me, were 'I love you.' We were taking the kids to the zoo. They were so excited. We all were, we hadn't been anywhere in a while. Half a second...in half a second, long enough to say, I love you, they were gone. I woke up a month later to find everything I ever knew...was...gone." I wiped my cheeks and looked back to Declan, who watched me with a somberness in his features I had never seen from him. "So, I sold everything and came to Scotland. I told my sister it was to find myself, but in reality, I think I was running away...away from the pain and the memories."

He reached his hand out to me. After staring at it a few seconds, I took it. "You can't run from pain and memories. You shouldn't. You need to hold on to them. Someday, you will want to look back and you won't be able to recall the face, the laugh, the good stuff."

I nod, knowing he is right. Wanting to avoid the emotions that were about to break through my walls, I shot out of my chair, "Would you like some tea?" Not letting go of my hand, he stood and embraced me.

"Gabriella, I am so sorry you had to suffer through that kind of loss. However, I am glad you were here for me. I can't bring your family back for you, but you being here, saved my life. And no, I don't want any tea, I think I am going to go lay back down a spell."

Chapter Twenty-Three

Gabriella

For five days Declan and I were stuck in my little house, although three of those he spent asleep. We weren't the American woman and the arrogant ass. We were just Gab and Declan. By the fourth day, he felt much better and his appetite returned. Keeping my thoughts to his medical status seemed to help curb the other feelings that simmered beneath the surface. The first night he arrived on my doorstep, he insisted as adults we could handle sleeping in the same bed. I was reluctant at first, but for whatever reason, I gave in and continued to sleep next to him at night.

That's not entirely true. I knew the reason but wasn't ready to admit it yet. I enjoyed lying next to Declan and liked waking next to him every morning. The third morning I awoke with him wrapped around me. During the daylight hours, we continued as if nothing ever happened. Nothing did happen, but holding each other held a level of intimacy we both refused to discuss. The fifth morning, I awoke alone. I looked out the window to see clear roads and vehicle tracks in the drive. I shook off the feelings of rejection. He wasn't mine to claim, nor did I want to lay claim to him. At least that is what I told myself.

About an hour after waking, the power returned. I plugged my phone in to charge. As it came back to life, a steady stream of texts began to ping in from my mom and sister. I made coffee and waited for the hot water to heat for a long shower and several loads of laundry. I didn't know when the next storm would arrive, but I needed to catch up on a lot before it did. As I loaded up the washing machine, I came across the clothing I took off Declan the night he showed up at my door. Checking the tags, I sorted them into their prospective piles and fought the familiar feelings of loneliness that tried to creep in.

Just before lunch, Hamish called, "Lass, I am making a trip into town would you like to go in?" I did and took the offered ride. We would be leaving in about fifteen minutes, enough time to do a quick inventory and make a list. I could also give Hamish Declan's clothing I just removed from the dryer to return.

Hamish drove in silence for about ten minutes of the ride before asking, "So, you and Declan got on alright I take it?"

I looked at him in horror. What kind of woman did he take me for? "We didn't do anything!" I spat out quickly and louder than necessary, feeling my cheeks heat.

Chuckling he responds, "Nay lass, that's not what I meant? You didn't argue, fight, or try to kill each other?"

"Oh." I felt like an idiot as my face heated with even more embarrassment, "then yes, we got on just fine. Actually, it wasn't as bad as I thought it would be. We talked a bit, but most of the time he stayed in bed resting."

"Aye, lass, he looked a wee bit peely-wally this morning. I can't imagine what he looked like a few days ago."

I shook my head, assuming he meant Declan still looked pale, "He was quite a mess." We fell silent for the rest of the trip.

∞ ∞ ∞

That night I put clean linens on the bed and climbed in. I lay there for several long minutes staring at the empty pillow, Declan's pillow. I rolled to the other side to face the wall, as I had done the past few nights. Finally, I turned to my back and stared at the ceiling, "You have to be kidding me." I slept over a year alone and became quite accustomed to it. Five nights with Declan Douglas in my bed and not even in a romantic way to boot, and I couldn't get to sleep. I tossed and turned for hours before finally falling asleep. When I woke, I felt sluggish, exhausted, and ready for a nap.

Chapter Twenty-Four

Declan

Three days after I went back home, I was packing to fly out again when Molly knocked on my bedroom door, "Declan is there anything I can help ye with?"

The usually talkative Molly had been quiet since my return from Gabriella's. "No Molly I think I got everything. I'm only gonna be gone for a few days then I'll be back." She silently stood in the door frame considering her next words I assumed. "Is there something you want to ask?

She fidgeted for a few moments before saying, "Ye look like hell Declan, but I couldn't help but notice your demeanor, well lad to be honest, you've been a wee bit surly in the past few days, did something happen with Gabby?"

I looked to my employee in stunned silence a moment. She had never in my adult life questioned me as such, "Well Molly, not that it is any of your concern, but no, nothing happened. Yes, I spent most of the time in bed, but as I told you, I was quite ill the entire time."

She let out a deep breath, "Declan, that lass has been through much and she doesn't need ye muddling up her head."

My mouth fell open, muddling her head? "Molly, you have known me a long damn time. Do you think I am the kind of man who would play games with a woman?"

She shook her head, "Nay, lad, I don't think ye are at all, but ye must know ye can't spend time in a woman's bed, sick or not, and something not change."

I stared at her a moment before going back to packing. She was right, but what she didn't know or even consider, what it does to a man to spend a week in a woman's bed while she cared for you, fed you, and bathed you for God's sake. Three days I have been back home in my own godforsaken bed and I hadn't slept at all. When I did fall asleep I would wake myself up reaching into empty air for a woman who wasn't even there. I slammed the lid on my suitcase and turned to Molly, "Nothing happened, nothing was attempted, and that will be the end of it. Do I make myself clear?" She nodded as I walked out the door and down the hall.

Chapter Twenty-Five

Hamish and Molly

"Did ye go down this morn and check on the lass?" Molly asked Hamish as they were sitting down to their evening meal.

Hamish took a drink before answering, "Aye, I did." He glanced back to his plate knowing full well his wife wanted him to elaborate on the topic.

"Well?" Molly harrumphs with growing impatience.

Hamish slowed in his chewing, knowing full well Molly was fixing to throw a fit. He swallowed and then looked to his wife to answer, "Well, the lass looked tired, but aside from that she was her normal cheery self."

"Do ye ken..." She started before Hamish cut her off.

"I don't think nothing of it. What I do ken is that ye need to quit readin' fables. This is the twenty-first century for cryin' out loud!"

Molly slapped her hand down on the table, "Twas not a fable I'd been readin', 'twere the writings left by Laird Robert Douglas to the future heir of this estate."

Hamish let out a disgruntled sigh, "Molly, my love, Robert Douglas wrote those words near five hundred years ago. He certainly was not known for visions or prophecies."

Molly stood from the table, shuffled off to their bedroom and returned with a stack of well worn, aged papers in hand. She sat back down, pushing her plate to the side and flipped to the page that she wished to see and began reading: "It came to me like a waking dream. The future of our great home. The stone and rock of days gone by is no longer but replaced by whitened wood. A woman with a saddened heart who speaks with a funny tongue stands in the circle clear upon the fae wishing stone. Her wish is to be free of the pain and have her heart healed. The Douglas who rules this land stands tall and proud like those before him, but he has hardened his heart to all those who come near. On the night of the winter solstice of his time, he will see a light that will guide him to his truest of loves. A love that will prove to be bound and blessed by the fae queen herself. The trials they have both overcome will bind them in the end."

Molly looked to Hamish as if what she had just read proved everything. Hamish shook his head, "I believe Douglas there got into a bad barrel of whiskey."

Molly stared at her husband incredulously, "Nay Hamish! Did ye ken the night Declan wrecked his Rover was indeed the winter solstice? He also saw a light which guided him to Gabriella. He told me himself, she claimed the lights were off, but he swore he could see it. What I don't know is if Gabby made a wish on the fae stone?"

"Woman, I think ye dipped into a barrel of bad whiskey yourself. The fae are an old Scottish myth. Robert Douglas did not foresee the future of the Douglas estate, nor did he envision Declan and Gabriella as the future of these lands."

Molly shook her head, "Ye can think what ye will Hamish, but Robert Douglas's letter also says for a time a great distance will separate them, but their love will not be denied, and she will return to her rightful throne."

Hamish having enough of the discussion stands from the table, "Well, should Gabriella leave and return, I may consider believing that tripe, but for now, I don't want to hear another word about it." With that, he left the table and prepared for bed.

Molly sat at the table staring at the pages before her. She turned the page to the sketch she hadn't shown Hamish. The two people in the drawing were being bound by a handfasting ceremony, whilst standing on the fae stone, in the circular clearing. Molly sighed, "If Douglas was off his rocker, he sure drew a striking resemblance of Declan and Gabriella."

Chapter Twenty-Six

Declan

I had been gone on business one full week when I finally returned home around nine o'clock on a Sunday evening. As I drove by Gab's cottage I tried to keep my eyes forward and on the road. However, I caught a dim flash of light out of my peripheral vision and turned my head to look. Darkness enveloped the small cottage and smoke rose from her flu, but no light came from inside the place. I turned my eyes back to the road and continued up the drive.

Arriving, I found the kitchen light on, but no one seemed to be around. A quick look around the empty room and I spied a note pinned to the refrigerator. "Declan, Molly and I went to Edinburgh for the birth of our grandbaby. We plan to return home Monday evening. Gabriella is aware of our departure and will keep an eye to the cattle in my stead. Hope you had a pleasant trip and Molly put a plate in the icebox if you are hungry. Hamish."

I wasn't hungry, I was exhausted. For ten days, ever since I left the care of Gabriella, I had hardly slept the entire time. I packed my single piece of luggage to my room and headed for my office with my briefcase. I sat at my desk not moving, staring at a blank computer screen. I didn't want to work, I didn't want to eat, all I wanted was a good night's rest. I considered my options. I could drink a bottle of my favorite scotch whiskey and pass out or take a couple of those over the counter sleep aides I picked up at the pharmacy, however neither option appealed to me. I had one other alternative, but I wasn't sure how that would play out. At this point, I had nothing to lose.

I stood up from my desk and returned to my room. Opening the suitcase, I found the parcel I picked up while in Las Vegas. I changed clothes, grabbed my coat, and headed down the stairs.

Chapter Twenty-Seven

Gabriella

I lay tossing and turning for the tenth night in a row. I hoped doing Hamish's chores today would wear me out enough to help me get to sleep. I even returned to the circle clearing, climbed atop the stone, and wished for a restful night's sleep. At this point, I would try about anything. I flopped to my side, staring at Declan's pillow for the millionth time and glanced at the clock, it was nearing midnight.

"This is getting to be ridiculous," I muttered to the empty space in my bed. At that moment I heard a light tapping at the front door. Hamish and Molly hadn't returned, and I didn't notice Declan drive in. "Who could possibly be knocking at this time of night?" I spoke to the floor as I made my way to the door. I flipped on the light and peered out the window to see Declan shifting nervously from foot to foot. Opening the door, I did a quick head to toes scan. He didn't look hurt and his new Rover sat out front. I took in his state of dress and caught myself before bursting out into a fit of giggles. He wore flannel pajama bottoms and stared at me like he was worried over something. Fighting back a smile, I manage to ask, "Declan, are you okay?"

He let out a breath before answering, "I can't sleep. I haven't slept well in ten days." He ran his hand over the top of his head. "Look, Gab, I know this is going to sound creepy and you'll probably think I have lost my mind...when I was here, I slept better than I have in years...and I..." He stumbled over the words as he tried to explain himself and having great difficulty finding the right way to explain, but I knew what he was getting at.

I opened the door and stepped aside to let him in. As I shut the door he turned to face me, "If you aren't comfortable with this, I do understand. I just...need some sleep!"

I studied his features for a few minutes. He did indeed look exhausted with dark circles under his eyes and pale pallor to his skin. If I were to be honest, he looked like I felt, it was time for honesty. "Declan," I began, but paused to clear my throat, "I haven't slept very well either and could use a good night's sleep myself."

He nodded, removed his coat to reveal a lightweight, short sleeve tee shirt, "I purchased pajamas on my trip. Don't know why, I didn't plan this, but..."

I smiled at his consideration and finished his sentence, "you won't be flopping around." He smiled back and nodded. Declan crawled into the spot he previously claimed in my bed and I got into mine. Without another thought or word, I fell sound asleep.

The next morning, I awoke feeling more rested than I had in days. I rolled over to find he was gone. The only evidence that last night ever happened was the fresh dent in his pillow. I stared at it for several minutes before getting up to do the chores. As I dressed for the day I thought about him showing up for an unscheduled sleepover. I wasn't entirely sure how I felt about it. Emotionally, I felt torn. I needed the sleep as well, but of all the people who could provide me with enough comfort to achieve a restful sleep, why did it need to be Declan Douglas? I then considered the man himself. How hard it must have been for him to knock on my front door and ask to sleep with me?

I snickered, "Oh, Diana, wait till our next phone call. I sure wish you would have chosen psychology because I have lost my ever-loving mind." I ate a bowl of instant oats and headed out to do the morning feeding and check on the cattle, pushing Declan Douglas from my mind.

∞ ∞ ∞

That night I sat next to the fire lost in thought, staring at my phone. My sister had been no help whatsoever. Matter of fact, she thought it was pretty awesome and started talking about cuddle clubs. Cuddle clubs! Where people pay other people to snuggle with them, hug them, or give nonsexual comforts. I didn't need a cuddle buddy, I needed to sleep...alone. I finished my cup of tea and glanced at the clock, nine thirty. I gave myself a few seconds to wonder if Declan would knock on my door again this evening before I headed to bed to try to find sleep.

Molly and Hamish returned late in the afternoon. I couldn't imagine him wanting to explain slipping out during the night and returning at the dawn's light. Not that we weren't both consenting adults, but admittedly, this situation is a weird one. Showing up at someone else's house, sleep with them, and then leaving without words ever passing between us. Part of me hoped he slept well last night and wouldn't return tonight. I crawled into bed and again found myself staring longingly at his pillow, tossing, turning, and feeling inexplicably frustrated.

Preparing to get back up and do word finds for a while, I heard the light knock at the front door. I didn't bother to look. I opened the door and stepped aside. This time, no words passed between us, I didn't need an explanation. We went to bed and fell asleep.

Two weeks into Declan's late-night sleepovers, I greeted him at the door as usual but handed him a key. I didn't need to get up and let him in. Clearly, he would continue to show up every night. He could just let himself in.

Chapter Twenty-Eight

Gabriella

Two months passed, every night Declan would crawl into bed with me, sleep, and be gone before I woke the next morning. Odd to say the least. What surprised me about this messed up situation, I never felt guilt, shame or remorse letting another man in my bed. Daniel and I discussed what we would do if the other died first. At the time, I told him I would never be able to move on, having someone other than him would be hard. I did feel that way, I couldn't imagine dating someone else, or spending my days with another man...except for Declan. I didn't know why I felt differently when it came to Declan, but him being close, made me feel...safe, comfortable, and complete.

We never discussed our arrangement. In the light of day, we were cordial with one another, but unless conversation called for it, we avoided eye contact with each other. I did my chores and he did whatever he did in his office.

Molly invited me up for Sunday dinner and I obliged. While the men were out of ear shot, she brought up the fact Declan would be leaving for a trip to New York for two weeks. He didn't mention it to me, but we didn't have that kind of relationship. I wasn't sure what we were doing, but his itinerary was not part of it. I notice Molly studying me carefully as if she thought I would react to this news, but I gave no reaction. "Well, I hope he has a safe trip and doesn't pick up another illness."

"Aye, lass, me neither. Ye ken, I've worked at the Douglas estate for many years and I never once remember Declan being that ill before." She stared at me with knowing questions in her eyes.

The way she said it gave me pause, "You don't think I made him sick, do you?"

She shook her head and chortled, "Nay lass, that's not what I meant at all. The lad works a lot of long hours. It was just a matter of time before it caught up with him. He was fortunate ye were in the cottage that night to save him. Ye ken, he hasn't been quite the same since that night. He seems to be in a much better mood and he doesn't look near as stressed as he used to."

I got the distinct impression she was prodding for information I wouldn't give freely. I shrugged, "Maybe his little accident caused him to reevaluate himself and how he lived his life."

Molly laid her soft, small hand over mine, "You might be right." She prepared to say more as Declan and Hamish came in to eat. We all ate in companionable silence before discussions began about cattle production, current market prices, and Hamish's considerations of all things about cows. I looked up from my plate several times to find Declan watching me as if he wanted to say something to me, but he always looked away. Hamish and Molly continued the conversation but occasionally exchanged knowing glances. After the meal Declan excused himself to go pack for his trip. I helped Molly clean up the kitchen and then headed home, to my cottage.

Chapter Twenty-Nine

Hamish and Molly

Molly stood in her darkened bedroom peering out the window. "Oh, will ye quit spying on the lad and come to bed," Hamish called from the bed.

"I tell ye, Hamish, every night, he slips out and goes down the drive to her cottage and returns before morning." She never took her eyes off the view from the window as she explained to her husband.

"That may be, Molly, but they're both grown. If he wants to slip off to see her every night, it's his business, not ours."

"Did ye ken he purchased pajamas? Declan hasn't worn pajamas since he were a wee lad."

Hamish shook his head, "What does that have to do with ye spying on him?"

"He goes down there to sleep. I don't think it is anything more than that."

"And again, I ask, what business is it of ours?"

Molly pointed to the window, "There he goes. He has his suitcase with him this time. His flight leaves early in the morn. Do ye think he is going to leave from the cottage?"

Hamish sighed in resignation, "Now that ye have seen him go, can we please go to bed?"

Molly turned from the window, "Aye, we can go to sleep now. I wonder how long they are going to keep this up?"

Hamish rolled to his side, "I for one hope they figure it out soon because ye are beginning to drive me quite mad with all this business."

Chapter Thirty

Declan

Of all the things I have ever done in my life this ranked as the strangest of them all. Sneaking out of my own house in the middle of the damn night to sleep with a woman, a woman who was also on my payroll. In essence, I paid her to sleep with me, which if that got out would be a major scandal even if it wasn't what it sounded like. What made it worse, sleep is exactly what we did. I found in the past several weeks I was growing fonder of Gabriella and the person she was. Watching her with Molly and Hamish made me reconsider my earlier judgments of her. Judgments made based solely on the fact she was an American.

Before leaving I dressed in the clothing I planned to wear on my flight and packed my sleepwear in my carry-on bag. I grabbed my luggage and headed for the front door. I let myself in with the key Gabriella gave me. I turned off the outside light, shut and locked the door. As I had done for the past few weeks, I checked the fire in the stove, adding wood if needed. After double checking the locks I took off my coat, grabbed my bag and slipped into the bathroom.

Most of the time when I arrived at Gab's I would get right into bed. Tonight, would be the first time I would change clothes first. I folded and laid my clothing on top of the dryer for tomorrow morning, put on my flannel bottoms and opted to forgo the shirt. I hated sleeping in anything at all, but felt I owed Gab that at least. Plus, on the selfish side, she had the tendency to roll over in her sleep and place her hand on my chest, something I would never admit I enjoyed.

Leaving the bathroom, I shut the light off before opening the door. Tiptoeing through the space on socked feet, I made my way to the bed and slipped in. Every other time, I fell asleep within minutes after my head hit the pillow, but I sensed an uneasy tension from my bedmate.

I rolled to my side and whispered, "Is something wrong?" She remained silent for several long moments, so long, in fact, I was about to roll over.

"What are we doing?" She whispered back.

I let out a sigh, "Honestly, I don't know."

"Why do you keep coming back?"

I thought about it a second before giving my answer, "After the first night, it just felt right to do it the next night. Most of the time, I don't think about it. I finish paperwork, clean up and head here." And that was the truth. It never crossed my mind not to go to Gabriella's.

"How long are you going to be gone?" She asked with a note of sadness in her voice.

"I have to stay for the entire meeting, so it will be next Sunday night before I am back."

She let out a heavy sigh, "I will miss you."

For a second, I was speechless. "You will? I figured you would be pleased to be rid of me for a few days."

She chuckled, but her voice almost sounded like she was crying, "This is all so strange, but in truth, I will miss you. I feel...I take comfort in you being here. I can't explain it."

I blew out a breath, "I know what you mean. I can't explain it either. It isn't rational or logical, but you aren't alone in this, I feel the same way being close to you."

She lay silent a few seconds before asking, "Is this all there will ever be?"

I thought about her question. Should there be more? This was an odd arrangement to be sure, but outside of sleeping, would we be compatible? Instead of answering her, I asked my own question, "Do you want to try to be more?"

"I don't know." That was all she said before I heard her breathing taper off into sleep. I stared at her shadowed sleeping form for several minutes before drifting off myself.

Chapter Thirty-One

Gabriella

Declan left the estate three days ago, which meant three nights of little to no sleep. Molly, kind woman she was, invited me up for supper all three evenings and I gratefully accepted, thankful for the distraction. Hamish discussed what would happen come spring and I looked forward to working again.

The fourth day of his absence I was helping Hamish clean out barn stalls when my cell rang. A highly unusual thing for me to receive phone calls during the day, so I slipped it from my pocket and looked at the screen, 'Diana calling.' "Hello?"

Her voice broke with a slight sob, "I need you to come back. Mom had a stroke and it isn't looking good."

My hand flew to my mouth and I felt faint, "Oh, no." Was all I managed to get out before she went on.

"She is in the room next to yours. If you could come back I could really use your support." I assume she meant in the room next to the one I had been in after the accident, but I didn't question her.

"I'll be on the next flight out and text you when I arrive."

"Please, Gabby, I really need you...now! I can't do this on my own!" She half cried.

"I know Sis, I'll be there as soon as I can."

I hung up and looked at Hamish who stared worriedly at me. "My mom had a stroke, I need to go home and help my sister. She said it doesn't look good."

Hamish reached out his hand to me, "Come on lass, let's go see Molly. She can get a hold of Tim, Declan's assistant. He will be able to make the fastest and best arrangements for ye."

Twenty minutes later, Hamish was driving me to Edinburgh to get on a flight from Scotland to New York. From there I would fly to Kansas City. Tim also arranged for me to have a driver with a car ready to pick me up and travel the two-and-a-half-hour drive to St. Patrick's Medical Center. I would be there within twenty-four hours. I had no idea who the unseen Tim was, but I must admit he worked miracles with travel arrangements.

∞ ∞ ∞

In twenty-eight hours I managed to arrive at my destination. I entered the hospital through the main entrance doors. The place, normally bustling with people, seemed to be empty. A little white-haired woman in a bright red blazer sat behind the information desk in the center of the huge room. I approached her, "Can I help you dear?"

"Ah, yes." The place held an eerie quietness I noted. "My mother, Gilda MacDonald was brought in, she had a stroke. My sister said she is on the fourth floor."

The elderly woman tapped a few buttons on her computer and then pointed, "Oh yes. Take that elevator there up to the fourth floor. Turn right and you will come to the nurse's station." Without a moment's hesitation, I headed for the bank of elevators she showed me. As soon as I stepped into the silver box with vivid red carpet, an odd sensation came over me. I felt...faint. The doors closed, and the car began an upward movement, then it jerked suddenly, and the lights went out. "Well, this is just great."

I stood in the darkness for several minutes before deciding to sit down. The enclosed space began to spin like a merry go round on fast forward. Relief filled me, knowing I was in the hospital because I felt like something was very wrong. Maybe I needed to eat. I laid my head back on the cool metal wall of the elevator and waited for help to arrive.

Part 2

Chapter Thirty-two

Gabriella

I must have passed out in the elevator. As I came to, I could hear a steady beep...beep...beep. What in God's name is that sound? My eyes flew open as realization dawned. Someone must have found me and admitted me. At once, I closed my eyes to the overwhelming brightness, "Turn the lights down," I hoarsely spoke to whoever sat next to me on the bed. I heard someone who sounded like my sister gasp at my sudden outburst of speech. I felt the bed shift a bit as the person stood and then moved across the room to flip the light switch. I again opened my eyes, blinking rapidly giving them time to adjust. The first thing or person rather, I saw was indeed, my sister. I half smiled at her as she began to weep, "You came back."

My smile faltered, "I told you I would. It took twenty-eight hours, but I am here. I didn't eat on the flight, I think my blood sugar may have dropped." Her mouth fell open and her hands trembled as she reached for me like she hadn't seen me in years. I pushed myself to a sitting position and noticed my muscles felt weak, like I hadn't used them in months. "How is mom?" Diana, whose face went pale, sat on the side of my bed staring at me, not answering. She looked...like she had seen a ghost. "Diana! You said mom had a stroke, is she okay?" Her entire body tensed at my question. She began sobbing incoherently, the only words I caught were 'didn't, what, and try.'

"Whose mom had a stroke?" My mother said as she came through the door. Now I was the one confused.

"Mom?" I glanced at my sister who still sat trembling and sobbing, then back to my mother.

"I'll go get the nurse." My mother sat the steaming cup of coffee down she held in her hand as she turned back out the door. I watched, perplexed as she left. Why would my sister lie?

"Diana?" I said quietly, "You called me yesterday afternoon and said you needed me to come back. You said mom had a stroke and it didn't look good." Her eyes filled with tears as she shook her head. "Why would you say mom had a stroke? I would have come home if you asked."

Still shaking her head, she stuttered out, "I only said that to try to get you to come back. Nothing else was working. I thought...if you thought there was a crisis, you would come back."

I felt my brows draw together as my healthy mother and a nurse walked into the room. The nurse spoke first, "Well, hello, how are you feeling?" She strapped a blood pressure cuff to my arm and turned the machine on.

"I feel a little woozy and weak. I haven't eaten since yesterday morning. I should have eaten on the flight, but I was concerned about mom." Three pairs of extremely confused eyes turned to me and Diana began loudly sobbing again.

The nurse spoke first, very slowly, "And what flight would that have been?"

I didn't know what difference it made, but I answered all the same, "I don't recall the flight number. I left Edinburgh, flew into New York, from there to Kansas City. A driver brought me the rest of the way." Then it occurred to me why she needed to know the flight number. "Oh no, was there some sort of virus on the plane? Was I exposed to something? I just assumed my blood sugar dropped. That doesn't happen often, but I have had a few spells in the past."

The nurse gave me a sad smile, "Gabriella, what day is it?" I thought about it a minute, with the time change and this blood sugar drop my memory felt fuzzy.

"Well, I believe it is around March eighteenth." I knew with certainty it was March, the exact day I couldn't be sure about. "It should be about Friday, I would think."

Everybody in the room stopped and looked at each other. "Okay, maybe it's Saturday. Let me think about it a minute." I begin working it all out aloud, "Declan left on Sunday. Monday, Tuesday, and Wednesday I had supper with Hamish and Molly. On Thursday, Hamish and I were mucking out the stalls when Diana called saying mom had a stroke." I shot my sister a dirty look for lying to me as I continued my process, "Declan's assistant managed to make fairly quick arrangements and unless I passed out in the elevator for longer than I thought, this would be Friday. I guess it could be Saturday too, if I managed to finally get some sleep."

While writing notes in my chart the nurse asked, "Do you know what year it is?"

"That I do know for certain. It is 2019."

The nurse straightened abruptly, "I am going to get the doctor." She darted for the door without another word.

"You two are acting extremely uneasy. What day is it?" I asked.

"It is Friday." Diana said in a whisper, "September the fourteenth."

My mouth fell open, "September!?" I exclaimed. "Dear God in heaven! What happened? I felt faint when I entered the elevator, but not like, I would pass out for six months."

My mother sat down next to me, "Gabriella?" She worried her lower lip before asking, "Who is Declan?"

I know my mother and I talked about Declan in at least four good conversations. Diana and I just discussed the weird sleeping thing Declan and I had going on. "Mom, you know who Declan is. He owns the estate where I have been living the past several months?" Maybe I never used his name in our conversations, "You know, the arrogant ass who hates American women?" They were still looking at me like they had never seen me before...I glanced at my sister, who looked as if she would bolt from the room at any moment. "I know you know who he is. The guy I have been sleeping with for the past few weeks." My mother gasped. I couldn't tell if my words shocked her or the fact I actually admitted it out loud. "Calm down mom, we were just sleeping. It's a weird situation. I talked to Diana about it a little over a month ago. Remember, you told me about the article you read about those stupid cuddle clubs?" I snickered running our conversation through my head, "You said there were people who hired themselves out to hold and cuddle strangers."

Diana sat down on the other side of my bed shaking her head, "I remember the article, but we didn't talk about it." She looked thoughtful for a few seconds. "You think you were in Edinburgh?" She sounded confused. What in God's name is wrong with these two?

I snorted, "No, I went to Dochas. My God did neither of you ever listen to a word I said when I called?"

Mom touched my hand. "Gabriella...do...do you remember Daniel?" I stared at her.

"Mom! What kind of question is that? Of course, I remember Daniel. Matthew and Jacob as well." She let out a breath.

Diana then spoke, "Do you know what happened? Do you remember the accident?"

"Of course I do. June seventh. How could I possibly forget something so horrific? What is with all the questions? Why have I been unconscious since March?" My level of agitation and confusion increased by the minute and with each alarmed look my family gave me. I was about to confront them on their weirdness, when Dr. Rodriguez walked in. "Hello, Gabriella, I am..."

I cut him off with a big smile on my face, "Dr. Rodriguez, I remember." He looked at me confused.

"I am. I'm sorry, have we met before?"

The smile fell off my face. I didn't have any clue what was wrong with all these people, but this situation was starting to feel like a bad B version of the Twilight Zone. "Yes, it has been almost two years ago. I was in a pretty bad accident. You removed my intubation tube and broke the news to me about my family dying." Everybody in the room went still, staring at me like I lost my mind.

My mother gasped, "Oh god in heaven," as she crossed herself.

Dr. Rodriguez lightly touched my hand, "That I did." He softly spoke. "And the nurse tells me, you just flew in from Edinburgh?"

I nodded. "I did. I came back after my sister called and said our mother had a stroke. I went to Scotland a little over a year after the accident to find myself and recover emotionally. They tell me I have been unconscious since March, what happened?"

The doctor nodded to the nurse, then ordered a CT scan and a full round of blood work.

"Why do I need a CT scan? Do you think something is wrong with me?"

He shook his head and looked to my sister, she nodded, the doctor stood and left the room. I looked back to my sister. "Gabby, it's only been three months since your accident with Daniel. You were in a coma ever since. You haven't been to Scotland. You haven't been anywhere, but right there in that bed."

I started laughing. That was the stupidest thing I had ever heard. "That's not funny. What, did you get a job here and decide to play a prank on me? I can't believe they would let you do something like that."

She shook her head, turned and grabbed a newspaper laying on the bedside table. She handed it to me, September 14, 2017, stamped clear in bold scripted font in the upper right-hand corner. I shook my head, "I don't understand. I went to Scotland, I live in a cottage on a large estate. I help Hamish take care of cattle and bale hay. Just a few months ago Declan was in an accident. If I wasn't there he wouldn't have survived." Then a thought occurred to me and my hand flew to my mouth, "Oh my God, if I wasn't there, he died."

My sister shook her head, "Gabby, he isn't real. Nobody died because you weren't there. This...Declan doesn't exist."

I crossed my arms over my chest like a petulant child. Taking in the view from my room window, "You, that doctor, mom, you all can say or think what you want. I know I went to Scotland. I saved a calf in the middle of a torrential downpour. I was shot at by a nutjob of a woman, and..." I could feel the anger bubbling up in me like red-hot magma about to erupt from beneath the Earth's surface, "Declan Douglas wrecked his Rover in November during a blizzard, barely making it my cottage. For three days, I took care of him. I bathed him, fed him, and slept next to him. Dang near every night after that I slept next to him! There is no way none of it was real."

My mother, picking up on my growing agitation sat down next to me, "Gabriella, it may have felt real, but I assure you. It was just a dream. You have been right here since June seventh. In November you, Daniel, and the boys started planning your vacation."

I huffed out a breath, "Mom..." I looked her square in the face, "I remember being in the accident with Daniel. For one month, I was in a coma. I went through hell trying to get myself back together afterward. I went to Scotland to escape the pain and to find myself, without my family. The accident you all claim occurred three months ago...happened almost two years ago in my mind. I grieved, I picked myself up, and had begun to move on. I don't have any clue what..." I waved my hand around in the air, "this all is, but I have already been through all of this. My heart, my soul is healed, thanks to my trip to Scotland and thanks to Declan Douglas." I could tell my little speech didn't even begin to penetrate either of them, as they were both looking at me like I had lost my mind. There was no point in arguing, so I went back to staring out the window in silent defiance.

About thirty minutes after the nurse left the room, she returned with a wheelchair to take me for the CT scan. My mind still turning around the thought, Declan isn't real. I never went to Scotland. I have been in a coma for three months. But it felt so real, Declan felt real! There is no conceivable way it wasn't...real. Over and over, I played the last year over in my mind, waking up, grieving, deciding to trek to Scotland, Hamish, Molly, and Declan. Nothing in my memory gave me pause, nothing screamed it was all a dream.

∞ ∞ ∞

The next morning, another doctor visited me. "Good morning Mrs. Fairmont. I am Doctor Jackson. Do you mind if I ask you a few questions?" She gracefully sat in the chair next to my bed.

"Ask away." I waved my arm through the air. Questions were all anyone wanted from me. I, for one, was sick and tired of all the questioning and awkward glances. Even my Mom and Diana were starting to treat me like a science experiment gone wrong.

She opens the file in her lap and crosses her legs, "They tell me you have been in a coma for three months. However, you believe you have been across the pond in Scotland. Is that right?" She tried to sound light and jovial, which only served to irritate me more.

"It seems you have all the facts. All I know is I was in a bad wreck, my family is dead, and I finally found peace and healing in Scotland."

She nodded thoughtfully, "Tell me about Declan Douglas."

I blew out a frustrated breath, "Declan. Well, let me see. He is probably in his early thirties, about six foot two or three, and very fit. Though I don't know when he has the time to work out." The last part more of a thought aloud to myself rather than a statement to the doctor. " He owns a large estate in Scotland and owns a successful real estate acquisition company." I chuckled before adding, "He doesn't like American women, but after I saved his life, he took a liking to me, I guess."

"What do you mean by, 'he took a liking to you?' Did you have a relationship with him?"

I scoffed, "Not exactly. We slept together, literally." Of the whole situation, this was the hardest to explain, especially to people who knew me. "After his accident, we were snowed in together for several days. He became terribly ill and I slept next to him to make sure he was okay throughout the night. While I am sure it sounds odd to most people, we both found we got a better night sleep next to each other than without. I guess you could say we had an arrangement of sorts. He would show up at bedtime and be gone before I awoke the next morning. To call that a relationship, would be a stretch. It was...I really can't explain it. It felt right, and it is what we did."

She stared at me blankly, "Are you aware...none of it happened?"

I narrowed my eyes at her, "If you mean do I realize to all of you it wasn't real. The answer is yes. But to me, in my heart, Declan Douglas was...is a very real man, who helped me to heal after the loss of my family. It may not have occurred in your 'reality' but it did happen." I gazed out the window for a few minutes then turned back to her, "What kind of doctor are you?"

She smiled mischievously, "I am a doctor of neuropsychology."

I snorted, "I am not insane. I know I was in an accident with my family. I understand I received several traumatic injuries. I also get everyone around me has watched me lay in a hospital bed for three months unresponsive, which means it isn't possible that I could have went to Scotland. I am a nurse, so I understand what you are trying to figure out. I can't explain to you what happened to me or how it was even possible, but in my heart, I know, without a shadow of a doubt, I went to Scotland. I met Declan Douglas and in the year I was there, I healed from the grief that consumed my life and found peace."

Doctor Jackson shakes her head in disbelief, "I believe you. I do, however, from a medical point of view I must ensure you are not a danger to yourself or those around you. Look, I won't take up any more of your time. You have a pleasant day Ms. Fairmont." Doctor Jackson left the room and I sat stewing over this latest situation I have found myself in.

Chapter Thirty-three

Dr. Jackson

Doctor Jackson made her way down the hall and took the elevator to the third floor, to her private office within the neurology department. Most cases coming across her desk were simple. Gabriella Fairmont's case, however, was the most unusual case she had come across in her thirty-five years of practice. The head trauma Gabriella suffered left no lasting effects the good doctor could ascertain, either from the CAT scan or with her one on one talk with the patient. Dr. Jackson made notes in the file laid out on her desk.

The patient conversed with no apparent stutter or break in communication. She appears very lucid and does not give the impression she is suffering from hallucinations or a disassociation with reality. Patient insists while she understands what she believes is not logical, in her heart, she honestly believes she spent the last three months continuing to live, which extended two years into the future.

The patient believes she interacted with a specific set of individuals, which I feel, in the best interest of this case, to contact those people to find out if they ever came in contact with the patient.

Doctor Jackson initialed the report, closed the file, and placed it in her current workload box. Leaning back in her chair, she considered for a moment, what course of action, if any she should take with Ms. Fairmont. She straightened in her seat and reached for her computer mouse, waking the screen from its slumber. She typed in her password and then pulled up her web browser, typing in DECLAN DOUGLAS, SCOTLAND.

Within three minutes of scrolling and skimming over news articles, the doctor felt more baffled by the situation. Tapping her pen on the arm of her chair in a steady thrum, she decided to call a colleague. Pulling her cell phone from her lab coat pocket, she went into her three hundred and fifty-three contacts in search of one. Glancing at the clock on her wall and a quick calculation, she was pleased it was only three in the afternoon where her former classmate and colleague worked, at Mercy General in Edinburgh, Scotland. "Well, goud day ta ye Lily. To what do I owe this pleasure?"

"Donald, can you tell me, does Mercy have a patient listed under the name of Declan Douglas?"

"Well, let me take a look here." He punched a few buttons on a keyboard before answering her question, "Aye. He's been here for quite a spell. Car accident about a year ago. His file says he was declared medically brain dead and taken off support." Doctor Donald Hammond muttered something under his breath. "If this report is accurate, when the physician removed the ventilation tube, the patient began to function of his own capacity. It says here, the lad woke up two days ago." He scoffed, "He woke, normal, but asking for a woman no one in his family seems to know. Why are you interested in Mr. Douglas?"

Dr. Jackson explained the eerily comparable situation with her patient, Gabriella Fairmont. Doctor Hammond stopped her mid-explanation, "Did you say Gabriella Fairmont?"

"I did. Why?"

"Well, I'm not too sure how to explain what is in my file here. Declan Douglas has been in an unresponsive coma following a violent car crash that killed his fiancé. However, the report reads, when he regained consciousness, he didn't ask for his fiancé. He asked for Gab and became irate with his live-in hired man screaming 'You hired Gabriella Fairmont! You ought to know who in the bloody hell I'm talking about!' Before you ask, yes, it is in this file as such. The nurse who overheard the exchange is fairly thorough in documenting her patients' conditions."

Doctors Jackson and Hammond continued their conversation for fifteen minutes discussing the patient files each of them held. "I tell ye what Lily, I have the rest of this afternoon free. I was going to go to the racket ball court with some friends, however I am intrigued with this and must say I am a little curious as to what Declan Douglas has to say about this. I'll head down there in a bit and get back with you this evening."

"Thank you, Donald. Like I said, the woman has a firm grasp on reality, other than this...I don't even know what to call it."

Dr. Hammond chuckled, "Peculiar, is what I call it. Sometimes, Lily, we have to look beyond the realm of medical possibilities and find our answers in spiritual happenings."

"There would have been a time I would have argued that point, but I must agree with you in this situation. I'll talk to you after a while."

Doctor Jackson ended the call with a myriad of questions than when she first found out Declan Douglas was, in fact, a real person in Scotland. She would definitely be interested to see what Mr. Douglas's response would be in return. Before returning to the stack of patient files on her desk, she decided to check her email while the computer was on.

Chapter Thirty-four

Declan

I sat statue-still in a chair looking out the window at the bustling late afternoon streets of Edinburgh below. I awoke two days ago, in a hospital bed back in Scotland, with absolutely no clue how I had gotten there. The last thing I remembered I had gotten into a car in New York City. At least three nurses and two different doctors repeatedly explained how I had ended up here, but I couldn't wrap my head around it. I tried, but she had been so real, her smell, her touch, right down to the way her ears turned red when she got angry. The staff, Hamish, and Tim, they could all talk till they were blue in the face, I would not accept it had been an illusion in my mind.

"Mr. Douglas?" A male voice called as he entered my room.

I turned to see yet another doctor in a white coat, "Aye, I am Declan Douglas."

He nodded as he moved into the room, taking a seat on the physician's stool tucked in the corner by the head of my bed. "I am Doctor Hammond, the on-call psychiatrist here at Mercy General."

I stared at him blankly for a few seconds before questioning, "And who, might I ask, requested your presence here?" These people couldn't be believed. Next, they would be placing me in a straitjacket and hauling me off to a padded room.

"A Doctor Jackson asked me to stop in and speak with you. Give my professional opinion on your...situation."

I stared at him for a few breaths then turned my gaze back out the window. "I am not crazy." I growled to the pane of glass.

"I am not implying that you are. Will you tell me what you remember?"

I turned back to him, "Where should I start?"

He shrugged, but asked, "Do you remember the accident?"

I hesitated a minute before replying, "I remember being in a minor incident, in the winter during a blizzard that almost cost me my life. I left my vehicle and walked to get help, which is why it was so bad. I barely made it, but I got to the cottage where Gab lived, and she saved my life. According to everyone here though, that mishap never took place, as a matter of fact, if they are to be believed, the date hasn't even happened yet. As for Tess's wreck...they tell me, I was in the car with her, however, I don't remember that. I remember her leaving and viewing pictures afterward of the scene, but not being in the collision itself."

Doctor Hammond stared at me a moment, "Since you have been awake has anyone shown you or talked to you about how the incident with Tess happened or appeared?"

"No."

He opened the clipboard he held in his lap, pulling out a file. "Can you describe the pictures you remember seeing?" he asked indifferently.

I closed my eyes, mentally picturing the images and began to relate in detail what I remembered seeing, right down to the bright red roses scattered along the highway. "I gave her flowers the morning she left, though I don't recall why. No one told me this, but I assumed the impact was so brutal the bouquet flew from the vehicle."

The doctor looked at me in stunned silence, blinked at me a few times, and then looked inside his folder. "The roses were white, not red and they spilled out of the floral delivery van that hit you." He fell silent a few moments before asking, "Can you tell me about Gabriella?"

I let out a long sigh, "What do you wish to know?"

He appeared thoughtful a moment, "What did she look like?"

Again, I shut my eyes visualizing her face, "She is about five foot two, maybe a hundred pounds. Her eyes are a beautiful shade of green with flecks of gold in them. Her hair is soft chestnut brown and cut short."

The doctor cut me off, "Does she have any distinguishing marks?"

"She does." I nodded, remembering the kitchen incident. "She has a scar that crosses her chest, from her shoulder to her hip. And another on her forehead which runs back into her hairline."

He stared at me open-mouthed a few beats, "Do you know how she got those scars?"

"I do. They were the reason she came to Dochas. She had been in a terrible accident with her family." I looked out the window again, "she was the sole survivor of her crash. Poor lass lost everything. She told me she came to Scotland to escape the emotional pain and memories."

I turned back to see him staring incredulously at me. "Well, Mr. Douglas, I think that is enough for today. I believe they wanted a recommendation for medication, but I don't think it is necessary." He stood to leave and glanced back over his shoulder, "Peace be with you, Mr. Douglas." And he walked out the door. I returned to looking out the window.

Chapter Thirty-five

Dr. Hammond

Doctor Hammond closed Declan Douglas's door when he exited. He walked with purpose down the hall to the waiting room where an older man silently sat awaiting his return. The weary man raised his head as the doctor approached, "Well, has the boy lost his marbles?"

Doctor Hammond shook his head, "He describes the scene of the accident with Tess to a tee, except he says the roses were red, not white and he insists he was not with her. He also detailed it as if he had a bird's eye view of it or looking at a picture of the event." He blew out a breath and opened his clipboard, "I can't explain that, nor this." He showed the old man a computer printed image of a beautiful young woman.

Hamish whistled, "She's a bonnie lass. Who is she?"

"This is Gabriella Fairmont of Missouri, the one he thinks he has been with. She was in a vehicular crash a little over three months ago and has been unresponsive as well. She awoke the same day, within minutes of Declan waking from his coma. I did not show him this picture, but he gave a good description of her, including the scars she received in her own crash." A look of guilt crossed his face before he went on. "This photo I swiped from her Facebook page and I also spoke with her physicians in the states. Due to the head trauma she suffered, they had to cut her long hair. Declan stated she has short hair."

Hamish shook his head in disbelief, "So, you are saying the woman Declan claims he spent a year with, does exist?"

The good doctor looked troubled for a moment before answering, "She not only exists but believes she lived a year of her life in Scotland with Declan Douglas even though she was only unconscious for three months and according to her family, has never been to Scotland." He looked to Hamish, "I am not going to medicate him. There is nothing in his behavior which warrants it. Honest to God, I really don't know what to think. If it were just him I would have chalked it up to a dream, but given the fact Ms. Fairmont is having the same issue..." He shook his head, "As a man of faith all I can do is leave it in God's hands. He evidently has a plan for these two which you or I am not privy to."

Doctor Donald Hammond left the old man even more unsettled than he had previously been. As he made his way down the hall, he quickened his step. He entered his office, locked the door behind him and placed the call to Doctor Lily Jackson. "Hello, Donald. What did you find out?" She answered sweetly.

Donald opened the bottom right-hand drawer of his large mahogany desk and pulled out a bottle of scotch and a tumbler. "I am not sure where to begin, other than to say, Declan Douglas absolutely believes he spent a year of his life with Gabriella Fairmont. Though he didn't say it, his body language when he spoke of her tells me he is quite fond of the woman." He took a sip of his scotch feeling the burn go down his dry throat.

"How is that possible? They never knew each other before, both were in a coma, and both believe she has been with him in Scotland? Donald, it isn't...well, that just sounds crazy."

"Aye, I will agree with you on that. It does sound crazy, but the fact is we both have patients who were both unresponsive to outside stimuli, who believe they were together during this time. It doesn't make sense to you, me, or anyone who knows these two I would imagine. I will tell you, I took a photo of Ms. Fairmont off her Facebook page. I did not show it to Declan, yet he described her perfectly. When I asked if she had distinguishing marks, he told me about the scars she received from her accident. The ones only you and I discussed a few minutes beforehand."

"I did some research while awaiting your call and came up with astral projection. Somehow they managed to project out of their bodies and find each other. According to what I read it could be in the realm of possibility."

Donald choked on the hefty sip he was about to swallow, "Astral projection?!?! Lily, you can't be serious? They'll laugh you out of the hospital for putting that in her records. I don't have a medical theory on this, however, something has happened to these two, but on another plane of existence. One we cannot see or understand. I am closing my file on Declan Douglas and might I suggest you do the same on Gabriella. These two have been through enough, they don't need two psychologists poking at them with sticks."

Chapter Thirty-six

Gabriella

After receiving a clear CT scan, perfectly fine blood work, and mentally stable evaluation, I could leave my room and wander around the hospital corridors. Making my way down a hall, I found a quaint little chapel with no one inside. I went in and knelt on the vinyl covered kneeler on the pew in front of me, quietly staring at the cross on the wall in contemplation. "It's been a long time since I have come to you, but I don't know where else to turn. Daniel and the boys are gone, and I accepted that loss a while back. Declan..." I pictured the man who I spent many hours with, whose life I saved, "is he real? Was it all simply the work of my mind? My heart tells me to go find him, he needs me...that I need him." Tears begin to silently fall to my clasped hands in front of me. "I found peace after losing my family. I can't..." I choked back the sob building in my throat, "I can't lose him too. I don't know what to do. Please, give me something. A sign to show me what I am supposed to do."

I don't know how long I knelt there in silent prayer before I heard a rustling of movement behind me and whispered voices. I raised my eyes from the red-carpeted floor to the wooden cross, before turning to see who entered the silent chapel. My heart skipped a beat as I took in three older men, dressed in traditional Scottish kilts, right down to the knee socks with...bagpipes? "Excuse me, lass. In about thirty minutes we are to play hymns in here. Do ye mind if we practice a wee bit beforehand?"

I blinked in rapid succession sure they were a hallucination. "You're..." I swallowed back the tightness in my throat, "you're Scottish?" I questioned like an idiot. Was this my sign?

"Aye lass, we are." The man in front grinned a toothy grin. He looked amused by my observation, but of course he had no idea of the complex messes my thoughts and emotions were in over the place he hailed from.

"Uh, sure I don't mind." I bobbed my head, still processing the fact Scotsmen were in this particular chapel, in the middle of Missouri. The chapel where minutes ago I had asked for a sign from God in.

They filled their bagpipes and began to play Amazing Grace. Divine intervention? I had no clue, but in my mind I had my sign. I would return to Scotland to find Declan Douglas. My heart said it was the right thing to do. My mind still was unsure. They played with such emotion my whole being swelled with longing. I need to find Declan as soon as possible.

When they finished playing the first hymn and started on the second I stood and silently slipped out of the room. I stepped into the elevator, my mind made up. As soon as I could check out of here and have my affairs in order, for the second time I would return to Scotland to find Declan Douglas and reclaim the peace that I once found. Stepping out into the brightly lit hallway of the fourth floor I caught sight of my sister standing at the nurse's station with a worried look on her face. She looked up as I approached, "Where in God's name have you been? I have been all over this place trying to find you. I thought you left."

"I went to the chapel for guidance." The lightness in my heart filled me with an excitement I couldn't explain, and I wouldn't let Diana take the little happiness I found away from me.

She visibly relaxed, "Did you find the answer you were looking for?"

I didn't miss her snarky, disbelieving tone, "As a matter of fact I did and even got a sign." She tensed with apprehension, "I am going to Scotland as soon as possible. There is a laundry list of stuff I need to take care of first, but I am going back." Judging from the look on her face she was going to argue with me, but I walked away heading for my assigned room to make my list. When she stormed into the room behind me I was pulling open the drawers trying to find paper and a pen. The tension coming off her filled every available space surrounding me, but I didn't give her my attention.

"Gabby? What kind of sign do you think you received? I turned to look at her, I noticed her jaw was tightly clenched as she tried extremely hard not to explode.

I blew out a breath, "Di, I asked for God's guidance, to send me a sign because I am at a loss as to what to do. Do you have any idea what happened?" She crossed her arms over her chest but didn't answer. "Scotsmen. Bagpipe playing Scot's entered the very chapel I was in to play hymns. Kilts and all, in the middle of Missouri! How many Scotsmen do you know living in this area? None!"

The room fell silent as she stewed in her own thoughts, so quiet I thought could hear the patient breathing in the next room. Before she spoke our mother walked in, "Girls? Is there a problem?"

Diana huffed, "Gabriella here thinks she had a divine intervention which has prompted her to go to Scotland to find this Declan guy."

My mother's face paled, "That's insane! You can't take off after what you have been through and search out a perfect stranger. Not to mention, he more than likely doesn't even exist. I am with Diana on this Gabriella, you can't do that."

I looked to my family in consternation, "Diana, look him up on your phone."

"What?" She looked stunned by my demand.

"Google him and see what comes up. Declan Douglas of Dochas Scotland." I crossed my arms over my chest this time in complete defiance.

Diana pulled out her phone and began tapping in the information. By the expression on her face, I knew she did it only to entertain my notion and wasn't expecting to find a thing, however, her face paled and she began to chew on her lower lip. Before I could get out a word, mom did, "Diana? Please tell me you didn't find anything."

"Is he real?" In my heart I knew the answer, but my mind was still having a tough time accepting the facts. Diana scrolled up, down, and back up again all while shaking her head. Without saying a word, she handed the phone to mom. Our mother's hand trembled as she went through the same actions Diana had taken. "Well? Are either of you going to answer me?"

Diana bit her lip and answered, "He's a real person. A wealthy businessman evidently. Other than global business news, the only other mentions of him is a bad car accident last year, but nothing else."

Mom piped up, 'It still doesn't mean anything Gabriella. The nurses would leave the TV on for background noise for you. Maybe your subconscious conjured him up like the article Diana read to you about the cuddle clubs. You thought she called you and told you, when she was sitting right next to you while you slept."

I shook my head no, I didn't believe that. "Is there a picture of him on your phone?" I watched as my sister tapped something and started to flip her phone around to show me. "Nope, don't show me." I closed my eyes and told everything I remember of Declan's appearance. "He is more than likely in khaki slacks, a white button down, with a maroon paisley tie and either wearing a navy-blue sports coat or it is slung over a chair behind him. He is very fit, like he works out regularly, though I don't know when he would have time for it." I half mused the last part to myself. "He is about six foot two, maybe three and has the most amazing head of dark brown, almost black, wavy hair that looks like it should have been cut two weeks prior to the picture. His squared jaw more than likely has a five o'clock shadow which looks quite attractive on him. So, how close am I?"

Mom's mouth hung open and Diana handed me her phone with incredulity in her eyes, "He's wearing a hunter green tie." I took the phone from Diana's outstretched hand and peered down at it. It was him, my Declan, exactly like I remembered him to be. They were getting ready to argue some more when a light tap came at the door and Doctor Rodriguez entered the room.

"Ms. Fairmont. Ladies. How are you feeling today?" He studied me intently.

"I feel just fine and would like to go home. I have been here for three months and have affairs needing to be handled."

He looked to my mom and sister, who I hoped would remain silent, but they didn't, "She thinks she received a divine sign and needs to go to Scotland."

Doctor Rodriguez worried his brows a second before turning back to me, "I would like you to stay in the hospital for one more night of observation and I would highly discourage you from taking any extended trips. Your CT scan didn't show any trauma, but that doesn't mean you are one hundred percent in the clear." His features softened a bit before he went on, "Could you wait four to six weeks, to be sure?"

I nodded my head in agreement, "Of course. I wasn't planning on jumping on a plane today. I will have to pack up my house, make changes to my financials, and sell my house. It isn't going to happen overnight." My answer appeased his concern. It didn't help Mom and Diana were making it sound like I was walking out of the hospital and boarding a plane either.

"All right then. I will have your paperwork ready first thing in the morning for your discharge. The process usually takes about an hour and you'll feel like a rock star after all the signing you'll have to do." He smirked, "We'll try to make it as fast and as painless as possible. Do you have any other questions?"

"No. I am just ready to get out of here and start my life." I wanted to add again, but I didn't want to push my luck. They still had a window of opportunity to lock me in a padded room. Doctor Rodriguez exited the room and my family turned on me.

Chapter Thirty-seven

Declan

Hamish entered my office but lost in my thought I paid him no mind. "Declan, lad..." I stared blankly out the window to the cottage down the lane. I hadn't slept in weeks and refused to take the sleeping medication the hospital prescribed. I knew what I needed...who I needed, but how to go about telling a strange woman I needed her to sleep with me? "Come now, let's go down and have a bite to eat."

"I'll be down in a minute." I woke up in a hospital bed six weeks ago. According to Hamish and Tim, I was in the accident with Tess and spent a year in a coma while my body recovered from the injuries I sustained. This is what they all said, but I swear she was real. I could still smell her skin, remember the warm touch of her hand on my bare chest, her smile, the way her ears turned red at the tips when she got angry. Memories like those and the person, the moments we shared, were too real to be a dream.

I stood from where I sat, grabbed my cane and moved to my desk. In the alternate reality, so I've come to refer to it, my house was much larger, given the fact the west wing had been added on, which housed my large home office and master bedroom. This room, a converted spare bedroom, seemed small and foreign to me. I would be remedying my issue soon by calling the contractor to build the addition I planned out well over a year ago. I turned on my computer to do a search I had put off because of fear, fear that what Hamish told me would in fact be true. She had to be real, she just had to be. I punched in her name like I thought had been done before. The article popped up, ' Tragic accident on Missouri Highway.' I read through the article, as I thought I already had done. It still read the way I remembered it. I pulled up her Facebook page. Everything I remember, except...something new graced her page. 'Gabby finally woke up today. She is a little confused but seems to be doing well. We are grateful for all the prayers. On a lighter note, she woke up thinking she spent the last three months in Scotland.' I stared at the screen, she thinks she has been in Scotland just as I believe, what were the odds. "Hamish!" I yelled. He came running up the stairs from the kitchen.

"What be the matter Declan?" He puffed, out of breath and panic etched on his reddened face, but I ignored his pained expression as I tipped my head to the screen.

"Look, it isn't just me."

He looks to the screen and then quickly looked to the floor. "Aye, I know lad." Remorse filling his voice. I paused in my motion to pick up the phone on my desk and called Tim to make flight arrangements.

Setting the handheld back on the base, "What do you mean you know?" I wasn't one to keep secrets and expected full honesty from my staff, more so with this situation.

"Doctor Hammond, the psychiatrist who visited with you, he received a call from a doctor who talked to your...uh...lady friend. The doctor was interested in seeing if you and the woman experienced the same things. I wanted to give you some time before I brought it up, afraid you would take off looking for her. You weren't... you still aren't in any shape to be flying across the country on a wild goose chase."

My brows drew together, and I shook my head whispering quietly, "That wasn't your decision to make."

"Declan, lad, Tim and I... well, we were concerned for your well-being. We wanted to protect you. We just got you back and didn't want to lose you again." I considered his point of view for a moment, letting the anger subside. Hamish had been in my families employ for over half of my life. In some moments he felt more like a second father to me and I knew he cared a great deal. "I appreciate your concern Hamish, I do, but I can't explain it in words except to say, I need this woman in my life. Some days this all is extremely hard for me to understand as well. Before the accident, I didn't realize it, but I wasn't..." how could I express this without sounding like a complete ninny, "whole." Whatever happened to me in that coma, being near Gabriella, made me...complete. Not at first mind you, but once she and I bonded, I felt at peace. I need to find peace, again. I need to go to her, talk with her, and find out if she feels the same."

Hamish shook his head, "Declan, she can't feel the same because it didn't happen. You didn't bond with anyone. You were in a coma."

This had to be the most infuriating situation in my life and frustrating to try to put into words. "I get it. I do. What you all don't understand is to me, in my heart, that woman, my Gab, is a real person. A woman who makes...made me complete. Now, regardless if real or in a dream, she and I shared something." I poked my index finger at the computer screen on my desk, "Clearly, she believes it too or she wouldn't have woken up believing she spent time in Scotland. I have listened to your concerns, but I am going to the states. I am going to meet with Gabriella long enough to discern if there is something there or if it was all, in fact, a vivid dream."

Hamish stared at me with sadness in his eyes before he clapped me on the shoulder, "Just be careful Declan and don't get your hopes up." He studied me a few more seconds before leaving the room.

I picked up my desk phone once again and called Tim, "I need you to schedule my transportation to America, as close to Stapleton, Missouri as you can." Tim, always resourceful said he would have it done in thirty minutes. I stood to leave my office to pack. What were the odds two people who never met, were unconscious but continued living their lives...together? As a businessman, those were the most ridiculous odds ever, but my gut told me the odds were in my favor.

∞ ∞ ∞

The next morning, I headed for Edinburgh Airport, not without a major sit down demanded by both Hamish and Tim two hours before I left the house. I again explained to them, with a little more emotion, so they would understand, my need to go see Gabriella. With stern looks of concern in their eyes, both hesitantly gave me their blessing before I crawled into my Rover, my original Rover, and headed out. I pondered that while I drove. Would the events in the 'other reality' happen? What if what I experienced was a premonition of sorts? If so, this trip to America would be a wild goose chase as Hamish and Tim claimed.

As I sat down in my first-class seat, my mind reeled with a variety of scenarios before deciding this may be the stupidest thing I have ever done. Aside from starting to fall for a woman! only to wake up and find out it never happened. My head began to ache with unanswered questions. When the stewardess passed I requested two shots of their top shelf whiskey. She probably thought flyers nerves to be the problem, which I wished it was. I needed answers to all the questions filling my head and Gabriella Fairmont would have those answers, at least I hoped she would.

I landed in two major airports, before boarding a small eight-passenger jet. Within thirty-two hours I drove away from KCI airport in a rental car, forty-five minutes from my destination. About thirty minutes into my drive I came upon a man walking alongside the highway. Two things caught my attention, no one stopped to offer him a ride, and even though his hair and beard made him appear to be homeless, his clothing looked impeccably clean. The man wore a white jogging suit with red stripes running down both legs and the arms of the jacket. It wasn't raining or too terribly cold, but something in my gut told me I needed to stop and at least offer him a ride.

Checking my rear-view mirror and finding no cars in the distance, I rolled down the passenger side window and pulled up next to the man. "Can I give you a ride somewhere?" He smiled brightly at me and I could see his teeth were as brilliant as the suit he wore.

"That'd be appreciated. I need to go to the next town." I unlocked the door to allow him access to my car. As he got in and buckled up, he chuckled, "Do you believe twenty-two cars passed me and not a single one stopped?"

"What are you doing out this far?" A reasonable question I figured since I didn't recall seeing a car broke down on the side of the road.

"Truthfully? I am doing research. Studies show today's society is less trusting and not willing to help a perfect stranger, even if they have the time or ability to do so. One of my parishioners dropped me off fifteen miles back and I began walking to see if anyone would pick me up."

"Aye, and someone did. So, you are a priest?"

"That I am, of sorts. My apologies, I didn't introduce myself first. My name is Father Mike. I oversee a church in town."

"None of your parishioners stopped, surely, at least one of them drove past you?" The man looked rough, but getting a good look at him up close, he couldn't be much older than my own thirty-three years. Through my peripheral vision I watched as he pulled off the mangy wig and beard to reveal a clean-shaven, well-groomed man.

"They would have if they knew it was me. Maybe it was a shady thing to do, but Sunday morning when I ask for a show of hands of who seen the man outside of town walking and I know several of them did, I will then begin my sermon on the parable of the Good Samaritan. Now, don't get me wrong, I don't want them to put themselves in danger, but aside from my hair, did anything in my appearance give you pause? You, after all, did pick me up."

I considered his question a moment. "I noticed your clothing, therefore, I believed you were safe to pick up, however, I didn't unlock the door until I could look into your eyes."

I could hear the smile in his voice, "Do you often pick up strangers?"

It was my turn to chuckle, "I must be honest with you Father, you are the first I have ever stopped for. I have been through something, still going through something...unexplainable. Maybe my situation gave me a new hold on life." I shrugged. I didn't know why I stopped, normally I wouldn't.

"Is this something you are having trouble with, spiritual trouble? Maybe I could offer some guidance or words of wisdom. Is it possible this was a divine intervention for your peace of mind in your problems?

I snorted, "God knows I need all the help I can get, but I am afraid you wouldn't believe my story. Heck, I have a hard time believing it myself."

The priest looked at his watch, "We have about fifteen minutes, try me."

Fifteen minutes and a thorough explanation later, Father Mike smiled ear to ear, "So you have been given a second chance at life. God must have big plans for you."

That was all he took out of my story. "I hoped for a little more than that." I gave a dry laugh.

"You were technically dead, they pulled the proverbial plug, but you fought the odds. While in your coma, you believe you met a woman, a woman you know for a fact, went through a similar ordeal. My brother, if that isn't God's plan in bold black and white before you, I don't know what it is. Maybe the angels will come down next and sing his praises to convince you. I believe when you are reconnected with your lady friend you will find you have found your one and only...your soul mate if you will. Only one person who deals in souls and that is the man upstairs. Well, I suppose the one downstairs does too, but in a much different way."

"I didn't think the Catholic faith taught such things. You make it sound as if our souls connected while we were unconscious."

"That is exactly what I am saying, you were soul bound to be together, and your physical bodies hadn't figured it out yet. Two people's souls, meant to be together, who under extraordinary circumstances found their match, which is a rare thing, especially in today's world. And to answer your other statement, I am not a Catholic priest. We are an offshoot, I guess you would say. Some people consider us a New Age Theology, others assume we are a cult. I was a Catholic Priest for five years but felt called to do something a little different with my life. I began my own church after my own accident. I spent a week in a coma and a passage in the bible spoke to me when I awoke:

"But all things become visible when exposed by the light, for everything that becomes visible is light. For this reason, it says, "Awake, sleeper, and arise from the dead, and Christ will shine on you." Therefore, be careful how you walk, not as unwise men but as wise, making the most of your time, because the days are evil."

"Ephesians chapter five, verses thirteen to sixteen. You were asleep, the sleep of the dead. God, his blessed Son, and all the angels and saints are smiling down on you, bathing you in their holy light. You, as well as your counterpart, have an opportunity not afforded to most. I teach my followers to make changes in their daily lives outside of the church, to let their light shine, to walk as Christ would have done, and illuminate the darkness that is consuming our population. It is not something you can change overnight, but one light at a time, we can make the world a brighter place. Do good things for one another, like you, picking up a stranger in need." He paused for a breath, "There is my church." He pointed out a two-story blonde brick building that looked like an old school house.

As I pulled up to the curb a very pretty, very pregnant lady stepped out on the sidewalk. "That is my wife, Rebekah. I... dreamed of her while I slept the sleep of the dead. Not like your experience, before you ask. About six months after I checked out of the hospital I left the Catholic faith and started off on my own. Two weeks later, Rebekah walked into the hall and down to my very core I could feel she was the one...that was four years ago." He opened the car door and started to slide out, but he turned back to me. "Don't let your heart be troubled or your mind confuse what you feel. Hand it over to God and He will guide you. Good luck...I don't believe I caught your name."

"Declan, Declan Douglas. And thank you." We shook hands and I drove off, now only about five minutes from my destination. I felt...lighter. Father Mike's words sent a vibration of relief through me like a tuning fork. He didn't judge me or think I was insane, instead he offered me hope that I was on the right track. He shined his light on me.

Chapter Thirty-eight

Gabriella

This was insane, absolutely nuts, but I was going. I had been out of the hospital over a month. For the second time, I packed up all of Daniel and the boy's belongings. This time I made the donations myself. For the people who knew me, they were confused by my lack of grief and upset. They didn't understand I had already grieved. I spent two years grieving and healing over the loss of my family. Mentally, I had already moved on and if I were being truthful with myself, Declan helped, Molly and Hamish as well. They were all very near to my heart even if they may not have known it.

As soon as we emptied the house I once again took up residence in my sister's spare bedroom. This time however, she acted like a hovering mother hen. She and mom must have made a schedule because I found one of them always with me. Most of the time they spent trying to talk me out of returning to Scotland. My heart and mind were both set on going and the only person that would be able to stop me would be God himself.

I put the house on the market and gave the agent the name of a 'potential' buyer. I gave my sister the legal power of attorney to sign all documents that were necessary in my stead and changed my life insurance policy to declare her my benefactor. Everything I thought was completed I did for a second time, with much less heartache this time.

I finished packing my suitcase when Diana tapped on the open door to my room, a pensive expression on her face. "Gabby, you can't show up on their doorstep. They will think you are insane. He isn't just some random guy, he is a wealthy and successful businessman." I think my sister thought our little online search of Declan would squash my desire to seek him out. All it did was prove me right and make me want to return to Scotland as fast as I possibly could, back to Declan.

. "Diana, I understand that, but you also read the article about his accident. This isn't random, stuff like this does not happen. Besides, I'm only going to find out if he remembers me, not declare my undying love for him."

My sister shook her head, "Sis, he can't remember you, you were never there." She whispers out as she leaves the room. I continued to pack, knowing this was the right thing to do.

∞ ∞ ∞

The next morning I boarded a flight in Kansas City with two layovers, but I should be in Edinburgh with in thirty-six hours. This time, I would be sure to eat on the flight or during one of my layovers. My trip from London into Edinburgh took forever, creating a growing anxiety in my heart. By the time I stepped off the plane I was second guessing my decision to come here. Rather than drive straight to the Douglas Estate, as my heart told me to do, I checked into a hotel for the night to think about what I was doing. Declan Douglas was in fact a real person and he did live outside of Dochas. What I didn't know, the kind of person he really was. All I had to go on was a subconscious dream that, at the time, felt real, so real, I constantly reminded myself that it wasn't. Even though I knew what occurred truly didn't, I still found it hard not to feel a deep all-encompassing need to be close to Declan Douglas.

I paced my room for a couple of hours before taking a shower and preparing for bed. Slipping under the sheets I sent out a little prayer, "Please guide me. I am so confused and lost. This all is so stupid, chasing after a man that I don't really know." I chuckled to myself as the thought of Samantha popped into my mind. Was I the crazy American woman stalking an unwelcoming Declan now? Definitely not. If he told me to leave, I would. The rejection would hurt, though it would be illogical. "Lord, this situation is so messed up." I rolled to stare longingly at the pillow Declan would be laying on if he were with me and let out a weighted sigh. Tomorrow, I would get the answers I so desperately need.

As I stumbled into the bathroom in the morning, I prayed silently the man I searched for wouldn't turn me away. As ridiculous as it was, I needed to sleep and I was about to the point of begging for just one night. I wondered in my sleep hazed mind if he was having difficulty as well. After I dressed, I packed my bag and headed for the coffee shop in the lobby. My heart screamed for me to hurry it up and get to the farm, but my brain still held me back.

Instead of rushing out, I forced myself to sit at one of the little tables the cafe provided. Staring into my coffee, intently watching the white cream swirl together with the darkness of the coffee, I did not notice the older woman who sat down across from me. I jerked back to reality, "I am so sorry, I was adrift in thought. Can I help you?"

She smiled warmly at me, "Nay lass. I wondered if I could help ye? Ye look... a wee bit troubled."

My brows drew together, "I'm lost, but not in a 'can't find my way around.' I am..." How could I explain this to a stranger without sounding like a nut job?

"Is it a boy that gives ye troubles? Sometimes, we must step back away from a situation to see the problem. If you are running, maybe it is a good thing."

I laughed, "It is a boy, but not in that way." I tried to give her a brief retelling of what happened to me and why I traveled here, leaving out who I was searching for and where.

She reached out with a frail hand and patted mine, "Ye been through much. I think ye are right in coming to find him in person. Ye don't want to go your entire life wondering what if. I didn't take that chance and have spent the last seventy-six years of my life questioning, what if I had sent that letter. My Gregor passed away sixteen years ago, he never married and to this day, I wonder, if I had mailed him the letter I keep in my nightstand drawer would we have found a way to be together? Now, I will never know. Don't fear taking a chance in life, especially when there is the potential for love. You may find yourself to be a ninety-eight-year-old woman stalking coffee shops looking for troubled souls to heal."

I smiled at her, "You're right. I have come this far, I shouldn't second guess my decision now. Thank you."

"You are welcome my dear. Now, finish your coffee and go find your young man."

I left the cafe, checked out, and headed for my car when I caught the sight of a lone, white dove perched on the powerline overhead watching me. For a moment I felt it was trying to tell me something, then I brushed that thought away. I was losing my mind, chasing dream men and thinking birds were giving me messages.

Chapter Thirty-nine

Declan

Pulling to the curb in a quiet residential neighborhood, I put the car in park and took in a deep breath. My heart began to pound as I realized in mere seconds I could be standing face to face with Gab. Sliding out of the driver seat, I composed myself and made my way up the front walk. I took in one more breath and knocked on a vivid red door of a quaint single-story ranch style home. A young woman answered, opening the door about an inch. She must be Gab's sister, she looked a lot like her, just a few years younger. "Diana?"

I wasn't a hundred percent sure I was at the right house, although, as soon as I spoke her eyes went wide, "Yes?" She opened the door all the way and stood open mouthed.

"My name is Declan Douglas, I am looking for Gabby Fairmont." She swayed as I said my name but steadied herself with a quick hand to the door jam.

"My, God, you're really real?" She studied me carefully.

I cleared my throat, knowing full well this woman thought her sister was crazy, "Is she here?" I asked firmly, not wanting to come across forcefully, but feeling the urgency growing, I needed to see Gab.

The woman before me shook her head, "She left for Scotland this morning...to find...you." She said the last on a whisper. "We thought she went insane...but...you're real...and you look exactly like she described you."

I looked out to the street as a car drove past before looking back to the woman before me. "Is she...is she okay?" I wasn't sure what to say to this woman who I knew had suffered through a lot with her sister. I didn't want to be short with her, but I needed to find Gab, the thumping in my chest was becoming unbearable.

Her voice quivered slightly as she responded, "I-I think she is." She looked relieved before her brows knitted together, "Are, uh, you okay? She asked, a little unsure eyeing my cane.

I answered her as honestly as I could, "I'm not sure. All I know is I have this..." I brought the palm of my hand to my chest.

Before I said another word, Diana did, "Overwhelming need to be close to her again." My mouth twisted in a pleased smirk, as she began nodding her head,

"Gabby, said nearly the same thing. I didn't want her to go in search of you. I feared it would end in more heartache for my sister. Clearly, I was wrong."

"My family felt the same way." I tried to make her feel better, knowing she wasn't alone in this mucked up situation. I smiled sheepishly at her and she grinned back. It was time for me to find my way back to Scotland, "Thank you for your time. I best be catching another flight." She just nodded her head and stared as I walked down the sidewalk to my rental car.

As I reached the door she called out, "Take care with my sister, will ya? She's been through a lot."

"I will." I assured her before sliding into my parked car. Before pulling away, I connected my phone to the available Bluetooth, so I could make calls while I drove back to the airport.

"Well, did you find her?" Tim, forgoing any pleasantries answered the call.

"I need you to make arrangements back to Scotland ASAP!" I ordered.

"Didn't go as you'd wanted? Sorry man, I know you had your hopes up." He sounded genuinely upset on my behalf.

"Nay, it didn't go as I had hoped, she is on her way to Dochas as we speak. She boarded a plane this morning."

I was met with a moment of silence, "You have to be kidding me? Well, at least there is some good news in that."

"What possible good news did you take away from that?" I was tired and getting irritated, usually Tim would take my orders, then take care of them, not dilly dally on the phone.

"You both are searching for the other." I heard the tap of keys through the line, "Looks like I can book you on a flight out of Kansas City at two this afternoon. You will have to board a plane in Chicago heading to New York. From there to London then your normal flight from there to Edinburgh. You won't have much of a layover time on any of those stops, so you are going to have to rush to make your next flight." I didn't care, I wanted to get home as soon as humanly possible.

"Listen, when I land in London I will call you. After all this traveling I will be exhausted. It would probably be a good idea if someone picked me up at Edinburgh. My Rover is in long term parking, so it shouldn't be an issue."

"Will do. All tickets are waiting at your gates. I will send the info directly to your phone."

"Thank you, Tim. You've been a wonderful assistant and I appreciate the work you do for me." He was silent, which was not surprising. I had never in the past ten years praised Tim for any of his hard work. That needed to change.

"You're welcome Declan, I'll see you in a few hours." I pulled out on the interstate heading back to Kansas City. After this trip, I decided I would slow down a bit.

Chapter Forty

Gabriella

The drive to Dochas, though only an hour, seemed to take an eternity. As I entered the town I found it looked exactly as I remembered it. This time though, the colors were as beautiful, vivid, and bright as I expected. I understood I had never been to Scotland, ever, but taking in the sights along the streets I couldn't fathom my mind conjured it all up. I drove on through Dochas and headed for the estate. Turning off on the lane that led up to the house I gave out a choked chuckle as tears filled my eyes. The driveway looked as I remembered it, including the large boulder which sat to the side marking the halfway point to the main house.

Butterflies began to churn in my stomach with the excitement of anticipation. "It had to be real. I couldn't have made this up if I wanted to." I say to my steering wheel. However, as I neared the cottage, my heart sank like a rock to the bottom of the ocean. The sight before me broke my heart. My cottage, my home, was in complete disrepair and the roof falling in. I pulled over, staring in abject horror at the overgrowth of weeds, broken windows, and the busted front door half hanging off the hinges, and wide open. Getting out of my car, my heart thrummed loudly as I gingerly walked up the rickety porch steps and through the doorway. I stepped into the living room, a chill of unease ran down my spine. The cottage floor plan was set up as I thought it had been, but no one could possibly live here. In all honesty, it needed to be torn down.

I was standing in the door frame of the bedroom staring blankly where my bed had been when I heard someone clear his throat. I slowly turned to see Hamish standing in the living room. "Are ye lost, lass?" he asked, a frown crinkling the skin between his eyebrows, then his face softened with...recognition?

"Hamish." I breathed out and his eyebrows raised.

"Aye lass, I be Hamish and who might ye be?"

I shook myself. He didn't know me because we never met. "I...I am Gabriella Fairmont." His face went white as a freshly bloomed lily when I stated my name.

"All the angels and saints, it can't be...you must be jesting?"

"No, I'm not. I'm..." I didn't expect this to be so awkward. Not sure what I expected, but this wasn't it. "I'm sorry, I am looking for Declan Douglas. Is he here?"

He stared at me for several long minutes, studying my face. I turned my face, so he couldn't see the scar that could be seen from his direct line of sight. Unlike in my 'other' reality, the scarring started below my eyebrow and went to the back of my head, giving me the appearance of a permanent part in my hair. It made me self-conscious for people to stare. "Declan..." He cleared his throat, "Declan went to the states to find...ye lass." He shook his head again, apparently confused by the situation. "Why don't ye come up to the house and have some tea."

My heart skipped three beats. "He's...looking for me too?" I couldn't believe it.

"Aye, lass. He woke 'bout a month back carrying on about his Gab. We all thought he lost his mind." He shook his head in disbelief. "But here ye be."

Listening to the man speak, I giggled quietly, but not enough. Hamish turned quizzical eyes to me, "Your Scottish brogue is a lot heavier than I remember."

He looked at me strangely for a moment before the smile that usually graced his face returned, "Is it a bad thing?"

I shook my head as he made our way to our vehicles, "No. It's just...it's well...strange."

Following in my car, I took in the familiar sights of the estate and finally, a peace settled over me, a peace of being...home. We pulled to a stop, my tranquility briefly interrupted, as I at once noticed the house Hamish led me to was not the same house that I visited before. This one looked to be much smaller. I slid out of my car scrutinizing the structure. After several minutes I decided the house was the same one, but it appeared as if part of it were missing. I moved to Hamish's side stumbling over my words in confusion, "What..." I wasn't exactly sure how to phrase my question. I paused considering how to verbalize my thoughts, "It doesn't look the same. There used to be another wing which shot out toward the west side of the main house. Declan's office and the master bedroom were located there. On the east side stood a beautiful conservatory with a water garden inside."

Hamish cast a sideways glance at me, "Declan had plans to build on before his accident if his business deal went through." He fell silent and I considered his words. In my false reality, I imagined Declan's house with an addition he had not yet begun, but did plan on building? If this whole mess wasn't strange to begin with that just put the proverbial cherry on top.

As we start toward the back door a man I didn't know stepped out, "There you are old man, I have been looking everywhere for you. Declan called yesterday, he is on his way back. The lass has already..." his words stopped when he caught sight of me, "left." He watched me with mystified shock as he crossed the distance to me,

"Holy Mary Mother of God. You aren't...are you?" He looked to Hamish whose face took on a pained expression. "Gabriella? Are you the woman Declan is trying to find?"

I nodded my head as a momentary sense of panic filled me, "I guess I am. He...he is looking for me?" My heart leaps at the thought.

"He was, but it looks like we found you first. I would call him back, but he is in London preparing to board a flight to Edinburgh." He studied me carefully. He glanced over my shoulder to Hamish, "He would like one of us to pick him up at the airport in about an hour." The strange man looked to me and then to Hamish, "I will go. I tend to drive faster." Hamish feigned hurt, then nodded as the man walked to a truck in the drive I never saw before. "Come on in lass, I will make you a nice cup of tea."

I followed him to the back door, a door I walked through many times. As we stepped on the porch I caught a flash of red out of the corner of my eye and ducked down jerking his hand as I went. "What on earth? Lass, what are ye doing?"

I lifted my head and peered in the direction of the red flash to only see another white dove flying off into the tree line. "I thought...I thought I saw..." Hamish stood running the palms of his hands through his silvering hair.

"What did you see?" curiosity and concern on his face.

How to explain an event which never happened without sounding nuttier than a Christmas fruitcake. I stood, and we went into the house, "Before..." I started, and he motioned for me to sit, "you must understand, I was in a coma for three months. During which time I lived about two years, the majority of which were on this estate." He studied me, with some understanding in his eyes. "While I was here, a woman named Samantha tried to shoot me. She was wearing a red cloak or at least that is what I remember."

At the mention of Samantha, Hamish gaped at me, "Dear Lord in heaven. Samantha... well let's just say, is no longer a concern. She was the cause of Declan's accident, but she didn't survive." I took a second to process his words.

"She died?" Hamish lowered his head while I tried to wrap my mind around that fact. "Declan's accident, how long ago did it happen?"

"A little over a year ago. They declared him clinically brain dead and I made the decision to remove him from life support. The moment they shut the machines off he was supposed to pass." Hamish shook his head, "Instead, he began to breathe on his own and his brain activity returned, but he never woke up. The hospital staff were all baffled by the situation. They said there was not a documented case of someone being brain dead surviving. Not to mention, actually waking up...normal? Do ye ken what I'm sayin'?"

"I do. But, he is...normal?" I felt panic rising in my gut. "I mean, aside from the oddness of it all, he is the same man you knew before?"

Hamish nodded, "Declan is fine, mentally. Physically, the damage to his leg was fairly bad requiring him to use a cane to walk, but aside from that, the doctors say he is fine. Well, except for..."

He trailed off staring at me, "He continued to live, even though he was not?" I asked, and he nodded.

"Very strange indeed." He shook his head in complete disbelief.

Chapter Forty-one

Gabriella

We visited for a long while. He was interested in my experience, what took place, and how I remembered things, although he never spoke of what Declan went through. I didn't know if Declan didn't mention his experience or if Hamish wasn't sharing. He got up from the table, "Well I guess I better put the casserole in the oven. We'll be havin' a full table tonight."

I studied his back with confusion, "Where is Molly? Is she up at your daughter's? Wait, she hasn't had the baby yet, I forgot." I clapped my hand over my mouth.

He stood stock still at the counter before stiffly turning to face me, "Nay lass, my daughter hasn't mentioned being with child." His eyes narrowed, "How do ye ken Molly?"

I took in the pained expression of loss on his face that I knew all too well, before answering in a quiet voice, "She...before...she took care of the kitchen, the house, and the gardens. She was so nice to me when I was..."

Hamish shook his head, "Lass, my dear wife Molly passed away some years back. I guess near on ten years now. I miss her terribly."

I sat still, mouth hanging wide open, "That's not possible. I mean, well, how could..." my mind raced through everything. Every instance Molly and I shared. It was one thing to interact with all these people, living, breathing people, but to dream, or whatever happened, of someone who passed years ago? Then his last words sank in, Hamish missed his dear Molly. "I am sure you do. Molly was the captain of this ship and kept the house running." I could feel the stinging sensation of tears start to prick my eyes then realized I didn't really know if she done such things or not. "I mean...I guess..." I put my face into my hands feeling like a complete idiot.

His voice softened as he took in my own pained expression, "Aye, lass, she did do that. It took me near on two years to figure out all she done and where she kept everything. I've no idea what has happened, but ye seemed to have known my Molly very well. "

My heart ached with the pain of loss for the woman who had helped me so much. I flashed through my memories again of Molly when Hamish broke into my thoughts. "Lass are ye all right?"

I shook my head, "I...I can't believe she's gone. Being here, knowing someone who is no longer here. Some things are the same, while others are a lot different. You say she passed ten years ago, but for me, I saw her just a few months ago. It is...emotionally as well as mentally overwhelming."

"I am sorry lass. I can't imagine with everything you have been through that any of this is easy. Although I must say, Declan and you seemed to be taking this all rather well. The rest of us," he lowered his eyes to the floor and shook his head slightly, "we are having a time trying to keep up."

"I understand. My family is overly concerned with my mental health. Actually, I started to question myself." My eyes took in the back door as if expecting something, "Being here, knowing he is having the same experience, well...it makes this situation much easier for me to accept and I am sure the knowledge will put my family at ease, at least a little." As I completed my sentence, my heart began to thump erratically in my chest. Without conscious thought I raised my hand and rubbed the spot.

"Are you a' right lass?" Before Hamish finished his question, we heard a vehicle approaching the house. My heart completely stopped for two beats before beginning its thumping again. He was here, and panic consumed me. How would he be? Would he be the arrogant American hating ass he used to be in the beginning? Would he be the man who I nursed back to health and slept next to many nights? Or would he be someone altogether different?

The back door opened and the man I now knew to be Tim walked in making eye contact with Hamish immediately. Something unsaid passed between the two of them, but I tore my eyes away as Declan Douglas entered the kitchen. He was just as I remembered him, other than the highly polished cane he used to walk and the slight limp in his gait.

Our eyes met, and my breath caught in my throat. Declan Douglas, a very real Declan Douglas, took me in from head to toe before whispering, "Are you real?" I nodded. So many questions were whirling through my mind that actual words were eluding me at the moment. "Do you know who I am?" Tears began to prick my eyes and I froze in place. He was real, and I wasn't crazy. I knew I wasn't, but to be in this man's presence made all my claims truthful.

His body tensed as if he were holding himself back. His brows drew together as he took two steps toward me before asking, "Can I...can I touch you?" My eyes took in Tim and Hamish who watched us with rapt attention before going back to Declan's emerald green eyes. With a single nod of my head he closed the distance, wrapping me tightly in his arms. As soon as he touched me a white light burst in my vision and the past year with Declan played through my memory. He held me with such love and fierceness I hoped he would never let me go. I took in a deep breath of his scent, soap mixed with perspiration from hours of travel. At that moment a warmth spread through me, he felt like safety...like I was home.

We stayed in that embrace for several long minutes before Hamish spoke up, "So, I take it you both recognize the other?"

Declan pulled back and peered down at me, "You do know who I am?"

My eyes locked with his, "I can't explain it, but yes, I spent the last year living down the road in that cottage. Every night..." I moved my eyes away, suddenly embarrassed by the words I needed to speak.

"I have lain next to you at night to sleep. The only way I could sleep, being close to you." He concluded my thoughts for me.

"Yes. It was all so..."

"Real?"

I nodded. This was the strangest thing I had ever heard of! Hamish broke into our conversation, "Well if you two are done greeting each other, I am ready to put the meal on the table." We all sat down and ate a few minutes in awkward silence. I sat, eating with people I didn't know but knew all the same, apart from Tim. To break the silence I asked Hamish about the cows and if he managed to get the hay put up this fall. He paused with his fork halfway up and stared at me open-mouthed. "Lass, we haven't ran cattle on this place in years."

Declan wiped his mouth with his napkin, "Hamish managed the livestock until..."

Hamish spoke up then, "After Molly passed, I, well, didn't deal with that very well."

Declan's expression became troubled, "Was...you remember Molly being here?"

"Yes I..." Looking to Hamish apologetically, "I was quite fond of her and can't believe she is gone."

Hamish looked at Declan, "You didn't mention Molly being with you."

Declan moved his eyes to his plate, "I was so confused when I woke up. I never questioned Molly being present. When...in the other reality I came downstairs and she was in the kitchen making breakfast. In the back of my mind I knew her presence wasn't right, but I was so happy to see her again I didn't question her. After I woke up you and Tim were telling me that Gabriella wasn't real and I had been in a coma...I didn't think it was the time to bring up Molly being with me."

As Declan spoke I still tried to process the fact there weren't any cattle on the estate. I wondered what else was different. My mind overflowed with questions I was afraid to ask. Except one, "Has the cottage been in disrepair long? I mean, when I first came here Hamish told me that the prior year American backpackers moved in and you had a heck of a time getting them out. Which I guess would have been just a few months ago, if you wanted to get technical about it."

Hamish spoke first, "The cottage has gone down in the past ten years, like many things around here I am afraid."

"Through no fault of your own Hamish." Declan chimed in, "There were backpackers that showed up here about six years ago. The cottage needed some repairs at the time. By the time I got them out, the place was a disaster. The past five years Hamish made repairs as needed to the main estate, but I must admit we kind of moved into a bachelor pad lifestyle around here. After Molly passed, well, we all fell apart in one way or another. Would you like me to have a contractor fix it back up for you?"

A considerate offer to be sure, "No, that isn't necessary. I was shocked, especially since I believed everything happened in the past two years either way I looked at it." I felt like my words were as confusing as my mind was, twisting the thought around, but Declan nodded in mutual understanding of my conundrum.

Hamish and I cleaned up the dishes, then he announced, "I will go prepare you a room."

At that Declan declared, "She will sleep with me." Then as if he couldn't believe he said the words aloud he added, "If...never mind."

I stared at him. I understood exactly what he was thinking. For everyone around us the reality remained, he and I were strangers who never met. However, for Declan and me, we have known each other for over a year. Hamish went on, "I will prepare the room and if you choose lass, you may stay there." He went off to take care of the task and Tim claimed to have paperwork to attend too, leaving Declan and me alone in the kitchen.

"Would you like a cup of coffee?" I asked as I took a mug out of the cabinet. Before he answered I reached for the second mug. Declan, or my Declan anyway, always drank a cup of black coffee after his meal.

He watched me for a moment before asking, "Tell me Gab, do I drink coffee?"

I turned to face him, pouring coffee into both mugs. Picking them up I walked across the kitchen and sat the mug down in front of him. "You like to have one cup of black coffee before you retire to your office in the evening," I stated as fact because to me it was.

Declan grinned happily, "I indeed do like that. You prefer a mug with cream and two sugars." He pushed both containers on the table toward me.

I looked at the table, "That is correct."

He let out a heavy sigh, "I don't know about your experience, but for me it was so very real. They say I was in an unresponsive coma with no brain activity. When they took me off life support they didn't expect me to survive. I...I think that is

when the accident in the snowstorm occurred, the one...the one you saved me from."
He reached out across the table.

I placed my hand in his. I had no explanation, "It was so very real. You were so cold and then you became ill. For the first twenty-four hours I feared you wouldn't come around."

He squeezed my hand, "I can't explain what happened to the two of us, but somehow we managed to continue on, together. We experienced...everything together. Well, until we woke up."

I studied his face, "Where do we go from here? I realize that sounds extremely presumptuous of me, but I have a...connection to you...that I can't..." I couldn't find the words.

He leaned forward in his chair, "I want to keep going like everything did in fact happen. The night before I left, before we woke up, you asked me if there was going to be more. I am not going to lie, I need more. I need you to be with me."

I let out the breath I didn't know I held, "I need you too."

Chapter Forty-two

Hamish

Later that night Hamish laid in bed thinking over all the events that transpired over the past month. He spoke to the white tiled ceiling which had yellowed with age, "What do ye think of all this?" He blinked silently to the aged squares above his bed waiting for a reply, but none came.

Hamish let out a breath, "I don't know what to make of it. When I found her in the cottage she knew exactly who I was. At supper she talked to me about the hay and the cattle like we'd done it yesterday, when the alfalfa hasn't been put up on this estate in years. I never seen anything like it." He stared for a few seconds before continuing with the conversation. "And ye, there was no possible way she could have known ye or all the things you did here. She also knew where everything in the kitchen could be found. When she brought up Samantha I was shocked. Tim said nothing was released in the media or internet so there was no way for her to have knowledge of her either." Again, he listened for a reply that wouldn't come.

Hamish ran his hand down his face, "Honest to God Molly, I don't know what to think. She asked about ye and says Sarah is expecting or will be." He let out a heavy sigh laced with frustration as he shut off the bedside lamp, "Maybe I will pay Father Marcum a visit in the morn. He can provide some guidance to at least put my mind to rest. Good night my love."

Chapter Forty-three

Declan

Where did we go from here? The question Gab put to me weighed heavy on my mind. I thought back to the year we spent together as I stared out my bedroom window to where the cottage sat in darkened shadows. Many times I considered tearing it down, but I couldn't seem to bring myself to call the contractor. My great, great, great-grandfather built that cottage for his wife's sister in the early 1700's. I didn't know much of my family history except that the Douglas clan owned this land for many, many years, dating back to a time before William Wallace. We were a branch of the lowland Douglas's that held great power in the lower regions of Scotland.

I looked at my bedroom door and thought about Gabriella down the hall. I wanted to go be with her and she seemed to want to be with me as well, yet I was unsure. She looked, sounded, and smelled like my Gab, but that didn't make it her. I contemplated this several minutes and was about to go to her when a light knock came at my door. Upon opening it, I was taken aback by the most beautiful vision I had ever seen. "I...I can't sleep." She said softly. I opened the door to allow her entry and mused to myself, I always went to her, she never came to me.

"I'll be just a minute," I said to her quietly before turning for the bathroom. I slipped into my dressing room that had an entry from the bathroom, to retrieve my pajama pants. Opening the drawer, I became agitated at first. I hadn't washed my pajamas, nor put them away. Then realization dawned. I don't have pajama pants in this...reality. Moving to the next drawer down, I pulled out a pair of loose-fitting jogging shorts, deciding these would have to do. I moved back into the bath and began my nightly routine.

When I returned to the bedroom Gabriella was staring out the window at the cottage, as I had moments before. I moved up behind her and wrapped my arms around her. She leaned into my embrace as I took in a deep breath filled with her sweet vanilla scent. "Are you okay?" I spoke to the top of her head.

She was silent for a moment before responding, "I don't know. I am still having a hard time wrapping my head around this. What is real and what isn't? It is so...confusing."

I nodded my head but had nothing to say in response. Instead, I posed my own question, "Are you ready for bed?" I never asked her before. I would show up and we went to sleep. I chuckled slightly, and she turned in my arms to peer up at me with confusion.

"What's so funny?" A small smile started to form on her lips as she took in my expression.

"I was just thinking how odd it was that neither one of us questioned me showing up at the cottage in the middle of the night to sleep."

She shook her head, "No, I did question myself. During the time you stayed following your accident I had a tough time accepting that I was okay sleeping next to you. My heart told me it was okay, but my mind was still grieving for the loss of Daniel. When you started showing up, well, I had already become accustomed to sleeping next to you, it seemed it was the only way I was going to get any rest whatsoever."

"I questioned my sanity of sleeping with an employee. I remember on my way to the airport thinking how wrong it was to pay you to sleep with me even though that is exactly what we were doing."

Her brows drew together, and she asked, "How did you wake up? Four days after you left, I flew back to America thinking my mom had had a stroke. I passed out in the elevator and woke up. What happened to you?"

I thought about it a minute before answering her questions, "Those last days were a blur, almost like a dream. I remember waking up next to you and leaving for the airport. Next thing I knew I was sitting in a meeting in New York. I didn't feel well, so I hailed a cab to take me back to the hotel and I guess I passed out. The next thing I knew, I woke up in Edinburgh at Mercy General with Hamish sitting next to me telling me some cockamamie story about being in a car accident with Tess. The first thing I asked was where you were, and he had no idea who I was talking about."

She chuckled, "I know exactly what you mean. When I told them I thought my blood sugar bottomed out since I didn't eat on the flight from Edinburgh, my mom and sister gaped at me. I bet it took twenty minutes before someone actually filled me in. They tried to get me to see a shrink and I agreed, only if I could come here first. They are expecting me back in a couple of days."

I pulled her back to my chest and hugged her tightly, "I talked to your sister briefly."

She pulled back, "You did? What did she say?"

I laughed, "You should have seen her face when I said my name and she heard my accent. I was afraid she was going to have a heart attack. She was the one who told me you came to Scotland looking for me."

"They didn't want me to come. Understandable, I guess."

"I suppose. Hamish and Tim were against me coming to find you as well. I think they thought I was going to kidnap you and drag you back home kicking and screaming."

She let out a burdened sigh, "Nobody believes us. I don't fully believe it either, but I know what is in my heart."

I leaned down and kissed her forehead right beside the scar that began in her right eyebrow, "And I know what is in mine. Let's go to bed, we can figure out more tomorrow."

And, as we had done several times before, we crawled into a bed and promptly fell asleep.

Chapter Forty-four

Hamish

Father Marcum stared at me impassively for several seconds after I finished explaining to him why I came to see him. I finally broke the silence, "Have you ever heard such a tale as that?"

He shook his head, "Actually, I do recall something similar being documented in historical records." He stood from his desk and went to the bookshelf that stood dead center of the room directly behind his desk. However, he did not pull a tome from the shelf as I expected, instead he moved one of the bookends and the unit swung open to reveal a secret room.

"You mustn't tell anyone what I am about to show you. The items I have collected in here, well let's just say, some are banned by the church and would be destroyed or confiscated if discovered. However, they are historical, and I cannot bear to see them destroyed, even for the Holy Church."

"I won't tell a soul," I promised as we stepped into the room and the door shut behind us. Taking a look around, the room was quite large. Three of the walls held floor to ceiling bookshelves. The fourth wall, which we walked through, held huge locking cabinets. In the center of the room, a large oak table stood. At first glance, it appeared quite ordinary, but as I drew nearer I saw the top of the table held an intricate engraving that I would be able to identify anywhere, the Douglas coat of arms.

Father Marcum removed a key that hung around his neck and unlocked one of the huge cabinets. He opened the door to reveal artifacts, swords, scrolls, goblets, pendants, and many other items I couldn't name. He turned with a scroll in hand, "most of these items were given to my great-great-grandfather Marcum by Bernard Douglas to protect. Prior to my family acquiring them, the oldest Douglas son oversaw the antiquities of the Douglas line. Unfortunately, Bernard's only two children died before they reached their twenties. My family has kept the Douglas tradition of the oldest son taking charge of these items. When I decided to become a priest, my father made me swear that the items would come before the Church and that I would find the next protector." He looked to the scroll in his hand, "And I have kept my word except I must figure out what will become of these things in the future though, as clearly, I won't have an heir. I planned on contacting Declan and returning them to their rightful place, but then he was in that accident."

He laid the scroll on the table using iron weights to hold down the curling edges. I looked down at the parchment to see it written in Latin and dated 1602. Unfortunately, I was unable to read the written words. "Who wrote this?" I asked Father Marcum, who studied the text before us.

His eyes never leaving the page he spoke, "Declan Douglas." I let out a gasp as he went on, "the youngest brother of Robert Douglas."

"Robert Douglas, who had the vision?" I asked in shock.

Father Marcum nodded, "One in the same. There isn't much history on Declan Douglas other than what his brother, Robert documented, most claiming that he was quite mad. Just after his twenty-fourth birthday, his brother sentenced him to hang for suspicion of being a trader to the crown. On a separate parchment that depicts the hanging, it's written that Declan proclaimed his innocence and claimed it was his brother who was working against the crown, as well as delving into black magic. Shortly after the hanging, Robert Douglas gave his prophecy, saying his brother's misdeeds were going to lead to the downfall of the Douglas clan. What didn't make it into the history books...Robert Douglas named his brother as the restorer of the Douglas clan, or rather he named the future savior of the Douglas's as Declan Douglas. He doesn't specify that it is his brother." He glanced up as he finished his statement. My eyes went wide as saucers.

"I have never heard any of that. But, how does that fit into what happened to my Declan and Gabriella?" The little history lesson he gave me was interesting to be sure, but it still didn't answer my question.

Father Marcum straightened before speaking, "The Catechism of the Catholic Church states, ' The soul is the subject of human consciousness and freedom; soul and body together form one unique human nature. Each human soul is individual and immortal, immediately created by God. The soul does not die with the body, from which it is separated by death, and with which it will be reunited in the final resurrection.' In simpler terms when we die our soul returns to its heavenly home. It doesn't die, nor does it remain on this earthly realm. However, what the Church does not discuss or have sanction for, or any Christian based theology that I know of, is what happens to our soul when we medically die,but are brought back to life via modern medicine. That my friend is a very grey area. For example, Declan Douglas of the past was hung in 1599."

I looked at Father Marcum in stunned silence before glancing back down to the parchment dated 1602, "If he was hanged in 1599, how in God's name did he sign this three years later?"

Father Marcum smiled mischievously, "Declan Douglas didn't actually die until he was near sixty-five in the year 1640 and he died as Declan MacDonald. This parchment is his sworn testimony. I won't read it verbatim, but this is the gist of it. They did hang Declan Douglas in 1599, during a very cold winter. Due to the weather, the Scots of that time were unable to bury their dead, so they had a holding area, until spring. Douglas's body was placed in that holding area. He writes here, he watched from a bird's eye view, as his body was cut down and taken away.

He claims that he wandered, watching events unfold within the clan, for three days before he felt a pull. He says the next thing he knew he was with a lass and they built a home on a small parcel of land near the lowlands, raised six children and were quite happy for ten summers. He then writes, while riding to the closest market for supplies he became extremely tired. He stopped his horse for a break by a stream and fell asleep. When he awoke, he found himself in the holding area with the same five people who died all those years prior. Five full days after the hanging, Declan Douglas walked back into the keep, calling his brother a fraud and proclaiming all the deceitful things he witnessed from his brother. He was immediately escorted off Douglas land as the clan feared he had become possessed by a demon, to have returned from the dead. They were afraid to kill him for fear that the demon would leave him and take over one of them. He left for MacDonald lands to find the girl he had fallen in love with."

Father Marcum paused before going on, "The lass he believed he fell in love with was Bethany MacDonald. She too had been believed deceased after falling from her horse, but not much is written about her coming back to life, except that it happened. However, her clan believed it to be a blessing bestowed upon them by God himself. Declan Douglas reunited with her and joined the MacDonald clan. They had six children and lived on a small parcel of land until he passed in 1640."

I stared at the priest in shock, "So, this kind of thing has happened before? And to a Douglas no less"

Father Marcum nodded his head, "To a Declan Douglas. The Church will take no stance on it. I have never heard another story like it and would advise to not share it widely. While the times of hanging people or burning them at the stake have passed, stuff like this is still frowned upon."

I consider this for a moment before asking, "So what should we do?"

Father Marcum looked questioningly at me, "What can be done? Look at it this way, two people, spiritually connected, soulmates if you will, found each other. Were the circumstances in which they connected odd?" he shrugged, "maybe to you and me, but Hamish, if I have learned one thing in my sixty-two years, God has a plan for each and every one of us. I may not know it, but He does." He pointed toward the ceiling before going on, "I think Ecclesiastes chapter three verse one says it best, 'To everything, there is a season and a time to every purpose under the heaven.' Do not question God's plan. He has a purpose for how things have worked out between Declan and Gabriella. If you are concerned about this being the devil's work, I don't believe it is. Bringing two people together at a spiritual level really isn't his thing. Like the couple of the past, they transcended the realm of the living, found comfort in each other, then returned to our earthly plane to find each other again. It is unusual, to say the least, but beautiful all the same."

I chuckled at his statement and considered his words a moment, "Well, thank you for your time, Father Marcum."

"Before you go I want you to know that the late Declan Douglas, who later became Declan MacDonald, did a great many things for our country. Many people around here don't realize that he was originally a Douglas because it wasn't documented widely."

As I turned to face the door, something that had been niggling in the back of my memory pushed to the forefront, "Father? You said the girl from the past was a MacDonald?"

"Aye Hamish. Bethany MacDonald. Why do you ask?"

"Gabriella, I think, she was a MacDonald. That was her surname at birth. I recall seeing that name on Declan's computer screen."

Father Marcum considered that, "Is she Catholic?"

"I dunna ken if she is?"

Following the priest back into his office, he sat down at his computer and I stood across from him. "What was the lass's married name?"

I thought about Declan yelling at me after he awoke, 'For God's sake you hired her! Gabriella Fairmont, she was just here a few days ago!' "Fairmont. Her name is Gabriella Fairmont." The priest nodded and punched buttons on his computer. Within seconds he motioned for me to come around to his side of the desk.

"The Church has been pretty good about keeping records over the past couple of decades, even adding old paper records to our computer system. It looks like your two are not related, but both are direct line descendants of the previous Douglas-MacDonald clans. That is very interesting indeed." He remained silently thoughtful a moment, "I stand on my previous statement. This isn't magic, the result of a prophecy, or the devil's work. These two were, to simply put it, soul bound to be together. Let your mind be at ease Hamish, God knows what He is doing."

Chapter Forty-five

Declan

I awoke the next morning reaching for Gab, but she wasn't there. Surely it wasn't a dream. That would be the icing on the cake, a perpetual nightmare to be sure. I sat up on the side of the bed stretching to remove the stiffness that moved into my muscles while I slept. Slept. I slept like a babe last night, like I had once before. She was here...somewhere. I made my way to the bathroom to prepare for the day and search out Gabriella.

When I came out of the bathroom, a man in gleaming white robes trimmed in bright red satin ribbon sat on my bed. I was about to yell at him to get out of my room, but as my mouth opened my anger suddenly subsided. "I come in peace." He smirked, "As I believe is the common phrase in your time."

I gave an amused guffaw, I couldn't help myself, the man made a joke, which I got the impression was out of character for him. "Who are you?"

"My name is Sebastian. I am what your people commonly refer to as a guardian. More specifically, your guardian."

My mouth fell open, "Guardian? Like an angel from heaven guardian?"

He smiled, and his ice blue eyes lit up with amusement, "Yes, just like that. I have been given permission to show myself to you and explain what happened, so that you may find peace."

"Peace? Oh, hell, am I really dead and am not realizing it?" As if this wasn't confusing enough, now I had to deal with angels explaining the events of my life.

"No, you aren't dead. You are very much alive, and you are awake before you ask. If you will take my hand, I will be able to show you."

I hesitated and stared at his outstretched hand. I reached out and as soon as our skin touched I saw a fast-forward version of my life and all the times Sebastian was there to save me or help me, and there were a lot of occasions.

"Your eyes. I knew they looked familiar. I guess I owe you a thank you for all you have done for me."

He smiled, "It is my job. Your future is written, and it is of the utmost importance for you to continue. Let us sit and talk a bit." He motioned for me to sit in a chair that moments ago, had not been there. I sat to listen to what the man...angel, had to say.

Chapter Forty-six

Gabriella

I paced the floor in the room Hamish gave me in growing agitation, "Yes, I know you think I have gone completely off my rocker, but I am here, and he does remember me too!" I listened as Diana pleaded with me to return home. "I will come back long enough to close on the house and pack up some of my things, but I will be returning to Scotland. This is where I belong." Diana finally lets out a sigh that sounded defeated.

"Gabby, it may be cheaper to send the things you want to you. I will just send them and save you the money for two flights. Please, think about it first. I know you think you know him, but you don't."

I blew out a breath, "I understand you are concerned, but I swear, I am where I am supposed to be...I feel it, Diana." I knew this was hard for her and my mom both to accept, in their minds, they lost everything, got it back, only to have it all gone again.

Before hanging up I gave her a list of items that I would like to have and told her to just send them to the Dochas post office. I would go in this afternoon and make arrangements to receive the packages.

I found myself staring out the window again, but this time in the direction of the circle clearing, feeling an inexplicable pull to go to the stone. Without a second thought, I grabbed a hoodie from my bag and left the house. Within fifteen minutes I made my way through the trees to where I believed the clearing was. As I stepped through the tree line the golden rays of the sun broke through the thick clouds overhead. Immediately my eyes moved to the stone, dead center of the clearing. With the sunlight hitting it, it seemed to sparkle and glow with a magical quality I didn't notice before. I had made two wishes on that stone in my other reality, both granted. I asked for my broken heart to be healed and to be able to sleep.

I approached the stone cautiously as my eyes made a scan of the tree line for anything bright red or a weapon trained on me. Finding neither I placed my hand on the cool smooth surface. I didn't really have a wish, but I spoke, "I want nothing this time, I just came to see if you were real, if this place was as I remembered. Some things are the same while others are a shade different. You are much more beautiful in this reality." Maybe I was losing my mind talking to an inanimate object in the middle of a field.

As I finished my statement I caught movement in my peripheral vision. I looked up to see an older woman dressed in the whitest cloak I ever saw, trimmed in bright red, billowing around her in a nonexistent breeze. As I watched her approach, I found to my shock I didn't fear her, but felt that I knew her. When she was within six foot of me realization dawned, "I know you, you were in the hospital when I awoke...the first time. Her kind intense blue eyes looked directly into mine as she spoke, her words sounding like a soothing lullaby.

"My name is Rachiel and yes my child, I was there as I am always with you." I looked at her confused, but as she reached out for my hand and I took it, a flash of memories played through my mind. When I was six years old and about to chase a ball into the street, at ten when my father died, and I felt lost, when I married Daniel...she played the piano. Several other times where I was in imminent danger, sad, afraid, or lost...the old woman with the vivid sapphire eyes was there. Then flashes of after the accident, the waitress in the restaurant and then Molly. "I am, what I believe you cal, a guardian angel. More specifically, I am the guardian of your soul. This," she placed her hand on the stone, "has been called many things throughout time, but few actually ever come to understand its purpose. I like to call it the stone of Elohim. Only those, who are in need of guidance can see it. When you touch it the pain, need, or desires of your soul are brought to your guardian angel. If I can help, I will nudge you in the right direction."

My brow furrowed, "What if you can't help."

She shrugged, "That has never happened in the thousands of years that I have been in service.

"Why are you here now? Am I in trouble?"

She shook her head, "No child, you are not in danger and neither is Declan. When you touched the stone, I felt your soul was in turmoil over the events that have come to pass. Understandably so. I am here to explain what truly has happened to you.

She motioned for me to sit on a royal blue blanket that appeared on the ground. As I sat I asked, "This moment, this, time, is this...real or am I going to wake up again to find myself in a hospital bed again?

She laughed, and it sounded like thousands of birds singing in harmony, "This," she motioned with her hand to encompass everything around us, "is reality as you know it and live within it. In, for lack of a better word, the realm of angels and souls time has no meaning. Which is why you have memories of a time that never came to pass. Your soul continued to live and mingle with other souls on another plane." While her words were slightly confusing, I knew what she meant. "You, and Declan as well, both physically died but were brought back to the world of the living by the hands of exceptionally talented and faithful doctors. You see, when one passes, the soul leaves the body and eventually will return to its creator, God. It is already written, what the time and place is that your soul will leave your earthly body and move beyond the confines of this world. It simply, was not your time."

I remained silent, taking in her words. She continued, "What you and Declan suffered in your accidents, was tragic indeed. It was my fear for you, that if you and he did not find the other, your souls would be irrevocably damaged. You both have good souls, which the two together are complementary of each other. In order for your earthly mind to heal and keep your soul pure we decided to intervene. Rarely is such an occurrence allowed to happen, but what is written for your future, it became necessary for your meeting to come to pass. We intervened allowing the joining of your souls before you were ever physically conscious of each other."

"So, what he and I remember did happen, just not in a physical sense?" I was already having a hard-enough time grasping what happened to Declan and myself, but what she was telling me took it even deeper than what I could have imagined.

"Yes. You needed a way to heal and your heart desired to come to Scotland because that is where your other half resided. Declan had suffered his own heartache and loss. Even though he was reluctant at first, he was always destined to be with you and you with him."

She fell silent letting that sink in, so I asked, "What is written?"

Rachiel stood shaking her head, "This I am afraid I cannot tell you. We are allowed to intervene when absolutely necessary and under normal circumstances are not allowed to actually interact with our subject, let alone give an explanation." I stood, feeling for the first time since awakening, fully at peace with my life. "I will tell you, however, you are precisely where you need to be."

"Gaaaab!" I heard Declan yelling my name through the trees and turned to look over my shoulder in the direction of his voice. He made eye contact, smiled hugely, and began to try running in my direction. I turned back to Rachiel who was smiling at Declan.

"Peace be with you Gabriella and may the rest of your days be filled with happiness," she said to me as she touched my shoulder. Within a blink of an eye she was gone, replaced by two white doves with red tipped wings flying off into the sky.

"Peace be with you as well Rachiel," I whispered to the sky.

When Declan finally made it across the field to where I stood he embraced me, pulling me up off the ground and swinging us both in a circle. "I just had the most unbelievable visit!" I looked to the sky again, barely making out the two white doves circling overhead.

"An angel?" I asked as I brought my eyes back to his.

He smiled even bigger if it were possible, "Aye lass! You as well?"

Chapter Forty-seven

Gabriella

Declan and I agreed to never speak of the other time again or our visitors. It was too much to try to rationalize and even harder to try to give a plausible explanation to people who knew us. We didn't lie about how we meant, we just left out a lot of the details, focusing more on our future together. We went on about our lives, living in Scotland, having two children, and spending every day together for many years.

I never saw Rachiel again, until much later in my life, sixty-three years later, to be exact. I had become very tired and worn with old age, spending most of my days in bed. She appeared to me, looking much like she had all those years ago, "Are you ready my dear?" I nodded in silence. She touched her hand to my forehead. I closed my eyes. When I opened them, I was walking along a gravel road, no pain and feeling alive and...at peace. I had been here before, many, many years in the past. I look down the road to the light to see everyone who had gone before me standing in front of a brilliantly lit doorway. Daniel, Matthew, and Jacob, just as I remember them. My mom and my dear sister. Hamish and Molly. Then Declan stepped out from the brilliant light dressed in white robes with red trim and held out his hand. I took it and he smiled, "Welcome home, my love." And into the light we went.